THE FOLGER LIBRARY SHAKESPEARE

Designed to make Shakespeare's classic plays available to the general reader, each edition contains a reliable text with modernized spelling and punctuation, scene-by-scene plot summaries, and explanatory notes clarifying obscure and obsolete expressions. An interpretive essay and accounts of Shakespeare's life and theater form an instructive preface to each play.

Louis B. Wright, General Editor, was the Director of the Folger Shakespeare Library from 1948 until his retirement in 1968. He is the author of *Middle-Class Culture in Elizabethan England, Religion and Empire, Shakespeare for Everyman,* and many other books and essays on the history and literature of the Tudor and Stuart periods.

Virginia Lamar, Assistant Editor, served as research assistant to the Director and Executive Secretary of the Folger Shakespeare Library from 1946 until her death in 1968. She is the author of *English Dress in the Age of Shakespeare* and *Travel and Roads in England,* and coeditor of William Strachey's *Historie of Travell into Virginia Britania.*

The Folger Shakespeare Library

The Folger Shakespeare Library in Washington, D.C., a research institute founded and endowed by Henry Clay Folger and administered by the Trustees of Amherst College, contains the world's largest collection of Shakespeareana. Although the Folger Library's primary purpose is to encourage advanced research in history and literature, it has continually exhibited a profound concern in stimulating a popular interest in the Elizabethan period.

The Folger Library General Reader's Shakespeare

The Winter's Tale

by

WILLIAM SHAKESPEARE

WASHINGTON SQUARE PRESS
PUBLISHED BY POCKET BOOKS

New York   London   Toronto   Sydney   Tokyo   Singapore

A Washington Square Press Publication of
POCKET BOOKS, a division of Simon & Schuster Inc.
1230 Avenue of the Americas, New York, NY 10020

ISBN: 0-671-66917-6

First Pocket Books printing February 1966

16 15 14 13 12 11 10 9 8 7

WASHINGTON SQUARE PRESS and WSP colophon are
registered trademarks of Simon & Schuster Inc.

Printed in the U.S.A.

Preface

This edition of *The Winter's Tale* is designed to make available a readable text of one of Shakespeare's romances. In the centuries since Shakespeare, many changes have occurred in the meanings of words, and some clarification of Shakespeare's vocabulary may be helpful. To provide the reader with necessary notes in the most accessible format, we have placed them on the pages facing the text that they explain. We have tried to make these notes as brief and simple as possible. Preliminary to the text we have also included a brief statement of essential information about Shakespeare and his stage. Readers desiring more detailed information should refer to the books suggested in the references, and if still further information is needed, the bibliographies in those books will provide the necessary clues to the literature of the subject.

The early texts of Shakespeare's plays provide only scattered stage directions and no indications of setting, and it is conventional for modern editors to add these to clarify the action. Such additions, and additions to entrances and exits, as well as many indications of act and scene divisions, are placed in square brackets.

All illustrations are from material in the Folger Library collections.

L. B. W.
V. A. L.

June 1, 1965

Romance and Pastoral

In Shakespeare's age, men and women on all levels of society found pleasure in romances set in faraway lands where the characters engaged in fantastic adventures bearing no relation to everyday life. The most famous of the romances appealing to a courtly audience was Sir Philip Sidney's *Arcadia* (first published in 1590), which describes the true love of Prince Musidorus for Princess Pamela and of Prince Pyrocles for Princess Philoclea. But, in romances of this type, the course of true love never runs smoothly, and the adventures of the main characters lead to an infinite number of outlandish episodes, until the author loses himself and the reader in the complexity of the plot. Princes, princesses, kings, queens, shepherds, shepherdesses, huntsmen, knights, wizards, enchantresses, giants, fierce beasts, and anything that stirred Sidney's fertile imagination found a place in the tale. He was writing about a pastoral world of his own creation, based on his reading of late Greek, Italian, and Spanish romances, and he felt no compulsion to adhere to any geographical boundaries or historical realities. Shepherds sing of love in a rural setting where the weather is ever pleasant and the shepherdesses are always beautiful. But since love is often mingled with sadness, a melancholy strain haunts the melodies of Arcadia. Sidney's work, which circulated in manuscript for nearly a decade before its publication, was widely read and was influential upon other writers. Shakespeare, for example, got from it names for some of his characters in *The Winter's Tale*.

A variety of romances entertained readers in Shakespeare's day. Apprentices who might have found Sidney's *Arcadia* too rarefied for their taste had available such tales as *Guy of Warwick, Bevis of Hampton, Amadis of Gaul, Palmerin of England*, and scores of others. If the reading of chivalric romances turned the head of Don Quixote, the Englishman of Shakespeare's day stood in similar peril, for romances made up a large part of his light reading. Francis Beaumont and John Fletcher, the playwrights, satirized the popular appetite for plays based on romances in *The Knight of the Burning Pestle* (acted about 1607).

Shakespeare's audiences, whether they were habitués of the Globe or of the somewhat more sophisticated Blackfriars, were conditioned to the unrealities of pastoral romance. They did not expect situations to be "true to life" as they knew it in London or in rural England. They had read romantic tales of prose fiction; they had seen dramatized versions of pastoral romances; and they were ready to grant the illusions required of such imaginative writing. Shakespeare made frequent use of romantic pastoralism. Long before *The Winter's Tale*, in *Love's Labor's Lost, A Midsummer Night's Dream*, and *As You Like It,* he had employed motifs from pastoral romance.

Evidence points to 1610 or 1611 as the date of the composition of *The Winter's Tale;* it thus comes between *Cymbeline* and *The Tempest* and shares many of the qualities of these last romantic plays. Like *Cymbeline,* it is a tragicomedy. The irrational jealousy of Leontes, King of Sicilia, brings disaster upon his own royal house, disaster almost as inevitable as that in Greek tragedy. His queen, Hermione, is disgraced and apparently dies; his son and heir dies; his infant daughter is exposed to die; his closest friend, Polixenes, King of Bohemia, has to flee the Sicilian court; King Leontes' most trusted adviser, Camillo, in fear of his life, is obliged to follow Polixenes to Bohemia and to spend sixteen years in exile. Surely this is not the stuff from which an author can twist a comedy. Yet the conventions of romance are such that all—or almost all—comes right in the end. It is true that the young princeling, Mamillius, is never brought back to life and that one of Leontes' trusted lords, Antigonus, is eaten by a bear, but save for these sad mishaps everything ends happily. To achieve this cheering conclusion, Shakespeare has to invoke coincidences and conventions characteristic of romantic fiction and the drama based upon it. The spectators of *The Winter's Tale* did not regard these strange events as fantastic; such happenings were to be expected in Arcadia, or Sicilia, or even Bohemia, at least when imaginative writers wrote of these lands. Shakespeare could even give a seacoast to Bohemia without troubling

the spectators, for if any remembered that the real
Bohemia was as landlocked as Switzerland, they put
the thought aside; Bohemia in the play was merely
another province of Arcadia, whose borders and
seas were a creation of the writer's imagination.
Nobody got out an atlas to trace Polixenes' route
from Bohemia to Sicilia; it was enough to know that
kings and princes had passed that way.

Some modern critics have seen in Shakespeare's
last plays a use of myth and symbolism to convey
an allegorical interpretation of the meaning of life.
Shakespeare invested with meaning everything that
he wrote, and he obviously did more in *The
Winter's Tale* than merely to dramatize a romantic
tale; but that he deliberately and consciously set
out to create a systematic allegory is extremely un-
likely. To insist upon that kind of explanation of
Cymbeline, The Winter's Tale, and *The Tempest* is
to make Shakespeare a philosopher rather than a
dramatist. Within the framework of a romantic
play, Shakespeare touches upon philosophic con-
cepts and problems of life, but he is not preaching
a sermon.

In *The Winter's Tale,* Leontes' jealousy is the
cause of the potential catastrophes that follow, but
this play does not contain the profound study of a
tormented soul that we find in *Othello.* The reader
or the spectator of *The Winter's Tale* will not find it
easy to identify with Leontes, as he can with the
noble Moor. Leontes' emotion is too irrational, too
self-induced, to stir our sympathies and gain our
understanding. We feel that the great sin of the play

is Leontes' sin of hasty suspicion and unwarranted jealousy of a virtuous wife and an honorable friend. In the unfolding of the play, Shakespeare has Leontes go through a period of repentance, purgation, and expiation. In the end, when his expiation is complete, he recovers his lost daughter and discovers that Hermione, his wife, is still alive, and all presumably live happily ever after. Some critics have seen a common theme running through all three of Shakespeare's last plays, the theme of recovery of something lost, something precious regained through redemption, and in this persistent theme the critics discern a revelation of Shakespeare's serene optimism in his later years. Be that as it may, we must not lose sight of the fact that Shakespeare is first and last a practical dramatist and not a systematic philosopher. In *The Winter's Tale*, as in *Cymbeline* and in *The Tempest*, he is reflecting the new fashion in drama, a new taste for the romantic treatment of themes that a few years earlier would have demanded tragic conclusions.

The Winter's Tale, for all of its absurdities, is an interesting play that holds our attention. In reading a modern detective story where all of the tricks and devices are conventional and recognizable, we somehow manage to suspend our critical judgment and find amusement in the manipulation of the plot. In the same way, we allow the author of *The Winter's Tale* to gain our attention and to create an air of suspense while we watch the plot unfold.

If we find it hard to identify with Leontes, we

recognize in many of the other figures in the play human characteristics that appeal to us. Hermione, like other mature women in Shakespeare's plays, has a vivid personality that wins our sympathy. Actresses have found this role a satisfying one, though in performance the greatest actresses have not been content with absence from the stage from Act III, Sc. ii, until Hermione reappears at the very end of Act V. In Paulina, the outspoken wife of Antigonus, Shakespeare created a stage character who lives in our memory. Afraid of nothing, not even of the King's wrath, she defends the honor of the Queen until the last and gives Leontes a tongue-lashing that he deserves. In the last scene of reconciliation, when she has been sixteen years a widow, Leontes rewards her with the hand of his honest courtier, Camillo. Camillo himself is a stage type that Shakespeare was fond of portraying, the loyal, deserving courtier who remains true to what he knows to be right, even at the sacrifice of his own career.

Perdita, the young shepherdess, and Florizel, the Prince, are conventional characters in romance, but in *The Winter's Tale* Shakespeare breathes life into them and they become living personalities. Indeed, Perdita has been called the most charming of Shakespeare's heroines. Like Miranda in *The Tempest*, she has an artless appeal and an unaffected honesty in her love that distinguishes her from the coquetries and the sugar-candy qualities that frequently characterize the heroines of romantic drama. The role of Perdita has attracted some of the greatest actresses.

The high point of interest in the play is of course the sheep-shearing scene (IV, iv), upon which Shakespeare lavishes his greatest skill. Although it is presented with the conventional trappings of the pastoral, the scene transcends the artificiality of most pastoral episodes. One feels that here are real scenes of country life, that the old shepherd and his son are genuine country clowns, and that Autolycus is a fascinating rogue who really lives.

In the clownery which Shakespeare wrote for Act IV, he is at his comic best. His company obviously had an actor who was particularly good in the part of an old countryman, for Shakespeare manages to write that role into many plays. The old shepherd and his loutish son are an effective pair. The comedy role of Autolycus, the rascally ballad vendor, the "snapper-up of unconsidered trifles," is almost equal to that of Falstaff in its comic impact. Comedy is much beholden to Autolycus; his counterparts have been seen in many plays from that day to this. If we do not relish rogues in real life, we like the sublimated clownery of rogues as presented on the stage. In Falstaff and Autolycus, Shakespeare conceived two of the most entertaining rascals who ever wore greasepaint.

The atmosphere of the sheep-shearing scene breathes the fresh air of Warwickshire. One cannot help feeling that Shakespeare was putting into this scene his own delight in returning to country scenes that he had known as a boy, for *The Winter's Tale*

in all probability was written after the author's
retirement from active life in London. At fairs in
Stratford he had undoubtedly seen peddlers and
ballad vendors hawking their wares, in the manner
of hucksters everywhere. He had obviously listened
to the talk of shepherds and country wenches and
had relished their idiom. All of this he gets into a
pastoral scene in Bohemia, which might have been
fairyland—or Warwickshire.

Shakespeare may have been thinking of his own
garden at New Place in having Perdita name over
the flowers to Polixenes, Camillo, and Florizel in
the sheep-shearing scene:

> The fairest flow'rs o' the season
> Are our carnations and streaked gillyvors,
>
> . . . .
>
> Here's flow'rs for you;
> Hot lavender, mints, savory, marjoram;
> The marigold, that goes to bed wi' the sun
> And rises with him weeping. These are flow'rs
> Of middle summer.
>
> . . . .
>
> Now, my fair'st friend,
> I would I had some flow'rs o' the spring that might
> Become your time of day; and yours, and yours,
>
> . . . .
>
> Daffodils,
> That come before the swallow dares and take
> The winds of March with beauty; violets, dim,
> But sweeter than the lids of Juno's eyes
> Or Cytherea's breath; pale primroses,
> That die unmarried ere they can behold

> Bright Phoebus in his strength—a malady
> Most incident to maids; bold oxlips and
> The crown imperial; lilies of all kinds,
> The flow'r-de-luce being one.

This is no passage derived from bookish references but from remembrance of a growing garden such as Shakespeare cultivated in Stratford. The whole scene is one reminiscent of the country that the author, and many another Londoner, knew. It would have aroused nostalgic memories in members of the audience, just as it creates for us a vision of green fields and flowering gardens.

If *The Winter's Tale* had no other recommendation to justify it except the sheep-shearing scene, it would amply repay our reading. Indeed, that scene has been excerpted for presentation alone on the stage and has proved effective.

In style *The Winter's Tale* is less lyrical than the earlier plays and is filled with elliptical and sometimes rather cryptic expressions. This tendency to elliptical expression is characteristic of Shakespeare's last period. It also contains more prose passages than most of the other plays. Its complete disregard for the unities of time, place, and action violated one of the canons of the neo-classical critics of the late seventeenth and eighteenth centuries. In their opinion, the device of having Time serve as Chorus to announce the passing of sixteen years was a relic of an age of barbaric literary license. The use of a bear to devour Antigonus was also a violation of decorum that disturbed the critics. It is an odd piece of stage business. The dramatist did not need

a bear to help him get rid of Antigonus. One won-
ders if Shakespeare's company had a bearward
temporarily in its debt and used his trained animal
for a bizarre stage effect. Shakespeare's contemporaries were fond of trained animal acts, and
dancing bears were common. A bear is one of the
cast in the play *Mucedorus* (acted sometime before
1598 and again at Court in 1610). The extraneous
bear is one of the puzzles of *The Winter's Tale*.

The source of *The Winter's Tale* is a prose novel
by Robert Greene entitled *Pandosto, or, The Tri-
umph of Time*, first published in 1588 and reprinted
in 1607 with a new title, *Dorastus and Fawnia*. In
the novel the settings are reversed. The jealous
king is King of Bohemia and the offending friend
is King of Sicilia. Shakespeare rearranged some
episodes, changed the names of the characters (with
help from Sidney's *Arcadia*), and created out of
whole cloth the comedy of Autolycus and the
shepherds. Shakespeare may have got the statue
scene from the story of Pygmalion in Ovid's *Metamorphoses*, and some of the characters' names come
from Plutarch.

The Winter's Tale has had a long history on the
stage. It was probably first acted on the Blackfriars
stage, which Shakespeare's company began to use
as a winter playhouse in 1608-1609. Simon Forman,
the astrologer, mentions seeing the play, however,
at the Globe on May 15, 1611. Autolycus made an
impression upon him. After writing a brief sum-
mary of the play and mentioning the roguery of
Autolycus, Forman concludes: "Beware of trusting

feigned beggars or fawning fellows." Before 1640
eight performances of *The Winter's Tale* are recorded, seven of these being at Court. The play
obviously appealed to both popular and sophisticated audiences. It was one of the fourteen plays
presented at Court in 1613 during the festivities
celebrating the marriage of King James's daughter,
Elizabeth, to Frederick, the Elector of the Palati-
nate, who became King of Bohemia. The episodes in
which a king of Bohemia took part gave the play a
certain topical quality that may have accounted for
its selection.

When the theatres reopened in 1660, after being
closed for thirty-eight years under Puritan rule, a
new taste in drama prevailed, and *The Winter's Tale*
did not suit the cynical Restoration. No record of
its performance occurs again until 1741, when it
was revived at the theatre in Goodman's Fields and
again at Covent Garden. Slowly the play regained
its popularity. During the second half of the eighteenth century adaptations that emphasized the
sheep-shearing scenes were frequently seen. The
first of these, *The Sheep-Shearing, or, Florizel and
Perdita,* probably made by McNamara Morgan, was
an abbreviated version used as an "afterpiece" with
some other full-length play. It was transformed into
an operetta in 1761. David Garrick also made an
adaptation emphasizing the same elements under
the title *Florizel and Perdita*. Garrick's version was
often acted at Drury Lane, where Garrick himself
played the role of Leontes. At the rival theatre of
Covent Garden a somewhat longer version more

nearly like Shakespeare's competed for attention. Various other versions and adaptations found their way to the stage in the later years of the eighteenth century.

During the nineteenth century, *The Winter's Tale* was seen at frequent intervals, sometimes in abbreviated adaptations, sometimes in the original version or versions closely resembling Shakespeare's text. In 1802 John Philip Kemble revived the play at Drury Lane and a few years later produced it at Covent Garden. He played Leontes, with Mrs. Siddons as Hermione; their rendition of these roles received much praise from contemporary critics. For the next forty years, both Drury Lane and Covent Garden kept *The Winter's Tale* before the public.

The tendency of the second half of the nineteenth century was to emphasize spectacle in the performance of this play. Charles Kean produced it in 1856 at the Princess Theatre with the most lavish mounting an audience had yet seen. As interpreted by Kean, the play became an allegorical spectacle; gods and goddesses appeared in chariots, and the pastoral portions were elaborated into sylvan scenes as a romantic painter might have depicted them. The text of the play was lost in the kaleidoscope of shifting stage scenery. Unfortunately, Kean established a fashion for this type of spectacular representation, and *The Winter's Tale* suffered more than most plays from the attentions of the scene painters. A number of productions of the play occurred in the later years of the nineteenth century.

In this century *The Winter's Tale* has been seen

on the stage from time to time, but it is not one of Shakespeare's most popular plays. In 1912 Granville-Barker produced the play at the Savoy in an interpretation that attracted much attention, some favorable, some unfavorable. In recent years it has been seen in both Great Britain and in the United States. Peter Brook's production at the Edinburgh Festival in 1951 attracted much favorable comment. The Old Vic Company produced the play in Edwardian dress in 1955.

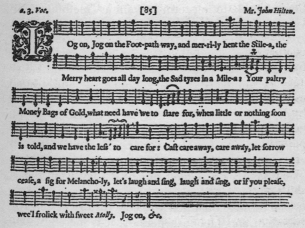

A seventeenth-century setting of Autolycus' song in Act IV, Sc. iii. From John Hilton, *Catch That Catch Can* (1667).

The first printed appearance of *The Winter's Tale* was in the First Folio of 1623, and it is upon that text that later editions of the play are based. The Folio version has fewer typographical and other textual errors than most of the plays and appears to have been printed from a carefully revised playhouse copy.

THE AUTHOR

As early as 1598 Shakespeare was so well known as a literary and dramatic craftsman that Francis Meres, in his *Palladis Tamia: Wits Treasury*, referred in flattering terms to him as "mellifluous and honey-tongued Shakespeare," famous for his *Venus and Adonis*, his *Lucrece*, and "his sugared sonnets," which were circulating "among his private friends." Meres observes further that "as Plautus and Seneca are accounted the best for comedy and tragedy among the Latins, so Shakespeare among the English is the most excellent in both kinds for the stage," and he mentions a dozen plays that had made a name for Shakespeare. He concludes with the remark that "the Muses would speak with Shakespeare's fine filed phrase if they would speak English."

To those acquainted with the history of the Elizabethan and Jacobean periods, it is incredible that anyone should be so naïve or ignorant as to doubt the reality of Shakespeare as the author of the plays that bear his name. Yet so much nonsense has been written about other "candidates" for the plays that it is well to remind readers that no credible evidence that would stand up in a court of law has ever been adduced to prove either that Shakespeare did not write his plays or that anyone else wrote them. All the theories offered for the authorship of Francis Bacon, the Earl of Derby, the Earl of Oxford, the Earl of Hertford, Christopher Marlowe, and a score of other candidates are mere conjectures spun from the active imaginations of persons who confuse hypothesis and conjecture with evidence.

As Meres's statement of 1598 indicates, Shakespeare was already a popular playwright whose name carried weight at the box office. The obvious reputation of Shakespeare as early as 1598 makes the effort to prove him a myth one of the most absurd in the history of human perversity.

The anti-Shakespeareans talk darkly about a plot of vested interests to maintain the authorship of Shakespeare. Nobody has any vested interest in Shakespeare, but every scholar is interested in the truth and in the quality of evidence advanced by special pleaders who set forth hypotheses in place of facts.

The anti-Shakespeareans base their arguments upon a few simple premises, all of them false. These false premises are that Shakespeare was an unlettered yokel without any schooling, that nothing is known about Shakespeare, and that only a noble lord or the equivalent in background could have written the plays. The facts are that more is known about Shakespeare than about most dramatists of his day, that he had a very good education, acquired in the Stratford Grammar School, that the plays show no evidence of profound book learning, and that the knowledge of kings and courts evident in the plays is no greater than any intelligent young man could have picked up at second hand. Most anti-Shakespeareans are naïve and betray an obvious snobbery. The author of their favorite plays, they imply, must have had a college diploma framed and hung on his study wall like the one in their dentist's office, and obviously so great a writer must have had a title or some equally significant evidence of exalted social background. They forget that genius has a way of cropping up in unexpected places and that none of the great creative writers of the world got his inspiration in a college or university course.

William Shakespeare was the son of John Shakespeare of Stratford-upon-Avon, a substantial citizen of that small but busy market town in the center of the rich agricultural county of Warwick. John Shakespeare kept a shop, what we would call a general store; he dealt in wool and other produce and gradually acquired property. As a youth, John Shakespeare had learned the trade of glover and leather worker. There is no contemporary evidence that the elder Shakespeare was a butcher, though the anti-Shakespeareans like to talk about the ignorant "butcher's boy of Stratford." Their only evidence is a statement by gossipy John Aubrey, more than a century after William Shakespeare's birth, that young William followed his father's trade, and when he killed a calf, "he would do it in a high style and make a speech." We would like to believe the story true, but Aubrey is not a very credible witness.

John Shakespeare probably continued to operate a farm at Snitterfield that his father had leased. He married Mary Arden, daughter of his father's landlord, a man of some property. The third of their eight children was William, baptized on April 26, 1564, and probably born three days before. At least, it is conventional to celebrate April 23 as his birthday.

The Stratford records give considerable information about John Shakespeare. We know that he held several municipal offices including those of alderman and mayor. In 1580 he was in some sort of legal difficulty and was fined for neglecting a summons of the Court of Queen's Bench requiring him to appear at Westminster and be bound over to keep the peace.

As a citizen and alderman of Stratford, John Shakespeare was entitled to send his son to the grammar school free. Though the records are lost, there can be no reason to doubt that this is where young William received his education. As any student of the period knows, the grammar schools provided the basic education in Latin learning and literature. The Elizabethan grammar school is not to be confused with modern grammar schools. Many cultivated men of the day received all their formal education in the grammar schools. At the universities in this period a student would have received little training that would have inspired him to be a creative writer. At Stratford young Shakespeare would have acquired a familiarity with Latin and some little knowledge of Greek. He would have read Latin authors and become acquainted with the plays of Plautus and Terence. Undoubtedly, in this period of his life he received that stimulation to read and explore for himself the world of ancient and modern history which he later utilized in his plays. The youngster who does not acquire this type of intellectual curiosity *before* college days rarely develops as a result of a college course the kind of mind Shakespeare demonstrated. His learning in books was anything but profound, but he clearly had the probing curiosity that sent him in search of information, and he had a keenness in the observation of nature and of humankind that finds reflection in his poetry.

There is little documentation for Shakespeare's boyhood. There is little reason why there should be. Nobody knew that he was going to be a dramatist about whom any scrap of information would be prized in the centuries to come. He was merely an active and vigorous youth of Stratford, perhaps assisting his father in his business, and no Boswell bothered to write down facts about him. The most important record that we have is a marriage license issued by the Bishop of Worcester on November 27, 1582, to permit William Shakespeare to marry Anne Hathaway, seven or eight years his senior; furthermore, the Bishop permitted the marriage after reading the banns only once instead of three times, evidence of the desire for haste. The need was explained on May 26, 1583, when the christening of Susanna, daughter of William and Anne Shakespeare, was recorded at Stratford. Two years later, on February 2, 1585, the records show the birth of twins to the Shakespeares, a boy and a girl who were christened Hamnet and Judith.

What William Shakespeare was doing in Stratford during the early years of his married life, or when he went to London, we do not know. It has been conjectured that he tried his hand at schoolteaching, but that is a mere guess. There is a legend that he left Stratford to escape a charge of poaching in the park of Sir Thomas Lucy of Charlecote, but there is no proof of this. There is also a legend that when first he came to London he earned his living by holding horses outside a playhouse and presently was given employment inside, but there is nothing better than eighteenth-century hearsay for this. How Shakespeare broke into the London theatres as a dramatist and actor we do not know. But lack of information is not surprising, for Elizabethans did not write their autobiographies, and we know even less about the lives of many writers and some men of affairs than we know about Shakespeare. By 1592 he was so well established and popular that he incurred the envy of the dramatist and pamphleteer Robert Greene, who referred to him as an "upstart crow . . . in his own conceit the only Shake-scene in a country." From this time onward, contemporary allusions and references in legal documents enable the scholar to

chart Shakespeare's career with greater accuracy
than is possible with most other Elizabethan dramatists.

By 1594 Shakespeare was a member of the company of actors known as the Lord Chamberlain's
Men. After the accession of James I, in 1603, the
company would have the sovereign for their patron
and would be known as the King's Men. During the
period of its greatest prosperity, this company
would have as its principal theatres the Globe and
the Blackfriars. Shakespeare was both an actor and
a shareholder in the company. Tradition has as-
signed him such acting roles as Adam in *As You
Like It* and the Ghost in *Hamlet*, a modest place
on the stage that suggests that he may have had
other duties in the management of the company.
Such conclusions, however, are based on surmise.

What we do know is that his plays were popular
and that he was highly successful in his vocation.
His first play may have been *The Comedy of Errors,* acted perhaps in 1591. Certainly this was one
of his earliest plays. The three parts of *Henry VI*
were acted sometime between 1590 and 1592.
Critics are not in agreement about precisely how
much Shakespeare wrote of these three plays.
Richard III probably dates from 1593. With this
play Shakespeare captured the imagination of Elizabethan audiences, then enormously interested in
historical plays. With *Richard III* Shakespeare also
gave an interpretation pleasing to the Tudors of the
rise to power of the grandfather of Queen Elizabeth.

From this time onward, Shakespeare's plays followed on the stage in rapid succession: *Titus Andronicus, The Taming of the Shrew, The Two Gentlemen of Verona, Love's Labor's Lost, Romeo and Juliet, Richard II, A Midsummer Night's Dream, King John, The Merchant of Venice, Henry IV (Parts 1 and 2), Much Ado about Nothing, Henry V, Julius Cæsar, As You Like It, Twelfth Night, Hamlet, The Merry Wives of Windsor, All's Well That Ends Well, Measure for Measure, Othello, King Lear,* and nine others that followed before Shakespeare retired completely, about 1613.

In the course of his career in London, he made enough money to enable him to retire to Stratford with a competence. His purchase on May 4, 1597, of New Place, then the second-largest dwelling in Stratford, "a pretty house of brick and timber," with a handsome garden, indicates his increasing prosperity. There his wife and children lived while he busied himself in the London theatres. The summer before he acquired New Place, his life was darkened by the death of his only son, Hamnet, a child of eleven. In May, 1602, Shakespeare purchased one hundred and seven acres of fertile farmland near Stratford and a few months later bought a cottage and garden across the alley from New Place. About 1611, he seems to have returned permanently to Stratford, for the next year a legal document refers to him as "William Shakespeare of Stratford-upon-Avon . . . gentleman." To achieve the desired appellation of gentleman, William

Shakespeare had seen to it that the College of Heralds in 1596 granted his father a coat of arms. In one step he thus became a second-generation gentleman.

Shakespeare's daughter Susanna made a good match in 1607 with Dr. John Hall, a prominent and prosperous Stratford physician. His second daughter, Judith, did not marry until she was thirty-one years old, and then, under somewhat scandalous circumstances, she married Thomas Quiney, a Stratford vintner. On March 25, 1616, Shakespeare made his will, bequeathing his landed property to Susanna, £300 to Judith, certain sums to other relatives, and his second-best bed to his wife, Anne. Much has been made of the second-best bed, but the legacy probably indicates only that Anne liked that particular bed. Shakespeare, following the practice of the time, may have already arranged with Susanna for his wife's care. Finally, on April 23, 1616, the anniversary of his birth, William Shakespeare died, and he was buried on April 25 within the chancel of Trinity Church, as befitted an honored citizen. On August 6, 1623, a few months before the publication of the collected edition of Shakespeare's plays, Anne Shakespeare joined her husband in death.

THE PUBLICATION OF HIS PLAYS

During his lifetime Shakespeare made no effort to publish any of his plays, though eighteen appeared in print in single-play editions known as quartos.

Some of these are corrupt versions known as "bad quartos." No quarto, so far as is known, had the author's approval. Plays were not considered "literature" any more than most radio and television scripts today are considered literature. Dramatists sold their plays outright to the theatrical companies and it was usually considered in the company's interest to keep plays from getting into print. To achieve a reputation as a man of letters, Shakespeare wrote his *Sonnets* and his narrative poems, *Venus and Adonis* and *The Rape of Lucrece*, but he probably never dreamed that his plays would establish his reputation as a literary genius. Only Ben Jonson, a man known for his colossal conceit, had the crust to call his plays *Works*, as he did when he published an edition in 1616. But men laughed at Ben Jonson.

After Shakespeare's death, two of his old colleagues in the King's Men, John Heminges and Henry Condell, decided that it would be a good thing to print, in more accurate versions than were then available, the plays already published and eighteen additional plays not previously published in quarto. In 1623 appeared *Mr. William Shakespeares Comedies, Histories, & Tragedies. Published according to the True Originall Copies. London. Printed by Isaac Iaggard and Ed. Blount.* This was the famous First Folio, a work that had the authority of Shakespeare's associates. The only play commonly attributed to Shakespeare that was omitted in the First Folio was *Pericles*. In their preface, "To the great Variety of Readers," Heminges and

Condell state that whereas "you were abused with diverse stolen and surreptitious copies, maimed and deformed by the frauds and stealths of injurious impostors that exposed them, even those are now offered to your view cured and perfect of their limbs; and all the rest, absolute in their numbers, as he conceived them." What they used for printer's copy is one of the vexed problems of scholarship, and skilled bibliographers have devoted years of study to the question of the relation of the "copy" for the First Folio to Shakespeare's manuscripts. In some cases it is clear that the editors corrected printed quarto versions of the plays, probably by comparison with playhouse scripts. Whether these scripts were in Shakespeare's autograph is anybody's guess. No manuscript of any play in Shakespeare's handwriting has survived. Indeed, very few play manuscripts from this period by any author are extant. The Tudor and Stuart periods had not yet learned to prize autographs and authors' original manuscripts.

Since the First Folio contains eighteen plays not previously printed, it is the only source for these. For the other eighteen, which had appeared in quarto versions, the First Folio also has the authority of an edition prepared and overseen by Shakespeare's colleagues and professional associates. But since editorial standards in 1623 were far from strict, and Heminges and Condell were actors rather than editors by profession, the texts are sometimes careless. The printing and proofreading of the First Folio also left much to be desired, and some garbled passages have had to be corrected and emended. The "good quarto" texts have to be taken into account in preparing a modern edition.

Because of the great popularity of Shakespeare through the centuries, the First Folio has become a prized book, but it is not a very rare one, for it is estimated that 238 copies are extant. The Folger Shakespeare Library in Washington, D.C., has seventy-nine copies of the First Folio, collected by the founder, Henry Clay Folger, who believed that a collation of as many texts as possible would reveal significant facts about the text of Shakespeare's plays. Dr. Charlton Hinman, using an ingenious machine of his own invention for mechanical collating, has made many discoveries that throw light on Shakespeare's text and on printing practices of the day.

The probability is that the First Folio of 1623 had an edition of between 1,000 and 1,250 copies. It is believed that it sold for £1, which made it an expensive book, for £1 in 1623 was equivalent to something between $40 and $50 in modern purchasing power.

During the seventeenth century, Shakespeare was sufficiently popular to warrant three later editions in folio size, the Second Folio of 1632, the Third Folio of 1663–1664, and the Fourth Folio of 1685. The Third Folio added six other plays ascribed to Shakespeare, but these are apocryphal.

PANDOSTO
The Triumph
of Time.

VVHEREIN IS DISCOVERED by a pleasant Historie, that although by the meanes of sinister fortune Truth may be concealed, yet by Time in spite of fortune it is most manifestly reuealed.

Pleasant for age to auoyd drowsie thoughts, profitable for youth to eschue other wuanton pastimes, and bringing to both a desired content.

Temporis filia veritas.

By Robert Greene Maister of Artes in Cambridge.

Omne tulit punctum qui miscuit vtile dulci.

Imprinted at London for I. B. dwelling at the signe of the Bible, neare vnto the North doore of Paules.
1592

Title page of Robert Greene, *Pandosto* (1592).

The theatres in which Shakespeare's plays were performed were vastly different from those we know today. The stage was a platform that jutted out into the area now occupied by the first rows of seats on the main floor, what is called the "orchestra" in America and the "pit" in England. This platform had no curtain to come down at the ends of acts and scenes. And although simple stage properties were available, the Elizabethan theatre lacked both the machinery and the elaborate movable scenery of the modern theatre. In the rear of the platform stage was a curtained area that could be used as an inner room, a tomb, or any such scene that might be required. A balcony above this inner room, and perhaps balconies on the sides of the stage, could represent the upper deck of a ship, the entry to Juliet's room, or a prison window. A trap door in the stage provided an entrance for ghosts and devils from the nether regions, and a similar trap in the canopied structure over the stage, known as the "heavens," made it possible to let down angels on a rope. These primitive stage arrangements help to account for many elements in Elizabethan plays. For example, since there was no curtain, the dramatist frequently felt the necessity of writing into his play action to clear the stage at the ends of acts and scenes. The funeral march at the end of *Hamlet* is not there merely for atmosphere; Shakespeare had

to get the corpses off the stage. The lack of scenery
also freed the dramatist from undue concern about
the exact location of his sets, and the physical relation of his various settings to each other did not
have to be worked out with the same precision as
in the modern theatre.

Before London had buildings designed exclusive-
ly for theatrical entertainment, plays were given in
inns and taverns. The characteristic inn of the period
had an inner courtyard with rooms opening onto
balconies overlooking the yard. Players could set up
their temporary stages at one end of the yard and
audiences could find seats on the balconies out of
the weather. The poorer sort could stand or sit on
the cobblestones in the yard, which was open to the
sky. The first theatres followed this construction,
and throughout the Elizabethan period the large
public theatres had a yard in front of the stage
open to the weather, with two or three tiers of covered balconies extending around the theatre. This
physical structure again influenced the writing of
plays. Because a dramatist wanted the actors to be
heard, he frequently wrote into his play orations
that could be delivered with declamatory effect. He
also provided spectacle, buffoonery, and broad jests
to keep the riotous groundlings in the yard entertained and quiet.

In another respect the Elizabethan theatre dif-
fered greatly from ours. It had no actresses. All
women's roles were taken by boys, sometimes re-
cruited from the boys' choirs of the London

churches. Some of these youths acted their roles with great skill and the Elizabethans did not seem to be aware of any incongruity. The first actresses on the professional English stage appeared after the Restoration of Charles II, in 1660, when exiled Englishmen brought back from France practices of the French stage.

London in the Elizabethan period, as now, was the center of theatrical interest, though wandering actors from time to time traveled through the country performing in inns, halls, and the houses of the nobility. The first professional playhouse, called simply The Theatre, was erected by James Burbage, father of Shakespeare's colleague Richard Burbage, in 1576 on lands of the old Holywell Priory adjacent to Finsbury Fields, a playground and park area just north of the city walls. It had the advantage of being outside the city's jurisdiction and yet was near enough to be easily accessible. Soon after The Theatre was opened, another playhouse called The Curtain was erected in the same neighborhood. Both of these playhouses had open courtyards and were probably polygonal in shape.

About the time The Curtain opened, Richard Farrant, Master of the Children of the Chapel Royal at Windsor and of St. Paul's, conceived the idea of opening a "private" theatre in the old monastery buildings of the Blackfriars, not far from St. Paul's Cathedral in the heart of the city. This theatre was ostensibly to train the choirboys in plays for presentation at Court, but Farrant managed to present plays to paying audiences and achieved considerable success until aristocratic neighbors complained and had the theatre closed. This first Blackfriars Theatre was significant, however, because it popularized the boy actors in a professional way and it paved the way for a second theatre in the Blackfriars, which Shakespeare's company took over more than thirty years later. By the last years of the sixteenth century, London had at least six professional theatres and still others were erected during the reign of James I.

The Globe Theatre, the playhouse that most people connect with Shakespeare, was erected early in 1599 on the Bankside, the area across the Thames from the city. Its construction had a dramatic beginning, for on the night of December 28, 1598, James Burbage's sons, Cuthbert and Richard, gathered together a crew who tore down the old theatre in Holywell and carted the timbers across the river to a site that they had chosen for a new playhouse. The reason for this clandestine operation was a row with the landowner over the lease to the Holywell property. The site chosen for the Globe was another playground outside of the city's jurisdiction, a region of somewhat unsavory character. Not far away was the Bear Garden, an amphitheatre devoted to the baiting of bears and bulls. This was also the region occupied by many houses of ill fame licensed by the Bishop of Winchester and the source of substantial revenue to him. But it was easily accessible either from London Bridge or by means of the cheap boats operated by the London watermen, and it had the great advantage of being beyond the authority of the Puritanical aldermen of London, who frowned on plays because they lured apprentices from work, filled their heads with improper ideas, and generally exerted a bad influence. The aldermen also complained that the crowds drawn together in the theatre helped to spread the plague.

The Globe was the handsomest theatre up to its time. It was a large building, apparently octagonal in shape, and open like its predecessors to the sky in the center, but capable of seating a large audience in its covered balconies. To erect and operate the Globe, the Burbages organized a syndicate composed of the leading members of the dramatic company, of which Shakespeare was a member. Since it was open to the weather and depended on natural light, plays had to be given in the afternoon. This caused no hardship in the long afternoons of an English summer, but in the winter the weather was a great handicap and discouraged all except the hardiest. For that reason, in 1608 Shakespeare's company was glad to take over the lease of the second Blackfriars Theatre, a substantial, roomy hall reconstructed within the framework of the old monastery building. This theatre was protected from the weather and its stage was artificially lighted by chandeliers of candles. This became the winter playhouse for Shakespeare's company and at once proved so popular that the congestion of traffic created an embarrassing problem. Stringent regulations had to be made for the movement of coaches in the vicinity. Shakespeare's company continued to use the Globe during the summer months. In 1613 a squib fired from a cannon during a performance of *Henry VIII* fell on the thatched roof and the Globe burned to the ground. The next year it was rebuilt.

London had other famous theatres. The Rose, just west of the Globe, was built by Philip Henslowe, a semiliterate denizen of the Bankside, who became one of the most important theatrical owners and producers of the Tudor and Stuart periods. What is more important for historians, he kept a detailed account book, which provides much of our information about theatrical history in his time. Another famous theatre on the Bankside was the Swan, which a Dutch priest, Johannes de Witt, visited in 1596. The crude drawing of the stage which he made was copied by his friend Arend van Buchell; it is one of the important pieces of contemporary evidence for theatrical construction. Among the other theatres, the Fortune, north of the city, on Golding Lane, and the Red Bull, even farther away from the city, off St. John's Street, were the most popular. The Red Bull, much frequented by apprentices, favored sensational and sometimes rowdy plays.

The actors who kept all of these theatres going were organized into companies under the protection of some noble patron. Traditionally actors had enjoyed a low reputation. In some of the ordinances they were classed as vagrants; in the phraseology of the time, "rogues, vagabonds, sturdy beggars, and common players" were all listed together as undesirables. To escape penalties often meted out to these characters, organized groups of actors managed to gain the protection of various personages of high degree. In the later years of Elizabeth's reign, a group flourished under the name of the Queen's Men; another group had the protection of the Lord Admiral and were known as the Lord Admiral's Men. Edward Alleyn, son-in-law of Philip Henslowe, was the leading spirit in the Lord Admiral's Men. Besides the adult companies, troupes of boy actors from time to time also enjoyed considerable popularity. Among these were the Children of Paul's and the Children of the Chapel Royal.

The company with which Shakespeare had a long association had for its first patron Henry Carey, Lord Hunsdon, the Lord Chamberlain, and hence they were known as the Lord Chamberlain's Men. After the accession of James I, they became the King's Men. This company was the great rival of the Lord Admiral's Men, managed by Henslowe and Alleyn.

All was not easy for the players in Shakespeare's time, for the aldermen of London were always eager for an excuse to close up the Blackfriars and any other theatres in their jurisdiction. The theatres outside the jurisdiction of London were not immune from interference, for they might be shut up by order of the Privy Council for meddling in politics or for various other offenses, or they might be closed in time of plague lest they spread infection. During plague times, the actors usually went on tour and played the provinces wherever they could find an audience. Particularly frightening were the plagues of 1592-1594 and 1613 when the theatres closed and the players, like many other Londoners, had to take to the country.

Though players had a low social status, they enjoyed great popularity, and one of the favorite forms of entertainment at Court was the performance of plays. To be commanded to perform at Court conferred great prestige upon a company of players, and printers frequently noted that fact when they published plays. Several of Shakespeare's plays were performed before the sovereign, and Shakespeare himself undoubtedly acted in some of these plays.

REFERENCES FOR FURTHER READING

Many readers will want suggestions for further reading about Shakespeare and his times. A few references will serve as guides to further study in the enormous literature on the subject. A simple and useful little book is Gerald Sanders, *A Shakespeare Primer* (New York, 1950). *A Companion to Shakespeare Studies,* edited by Harley Granville-Barker and G. B. Harrison (Cambridge, 1934), is a valuable guide. The most recent concise handbook of facts about Shakespeare is Gerald E. Bentley, *Shakespeare: A Biographical Handbook* (New Haven, 1961). More detailed but not so voluminous as to be confusing is Hazelton Spencer, *The Art and Life of William Shakespeare* (New York, 1940), which, like Sanders' and Bentley's handbooks, contains a brief annotated list of useful books on various aspects of the subject. The most detailed and scholarly work providing complete factual information about Shakespeare is Sir Edmund Chambers, *William Shakespeare: A Study of Facts and Problems* (2 vols., Oxford, 1930).

Among other biographies of Shakespeare, Joseph Quincy Adams, *A Life of William Shakespeare* (Boston, 1923) is still an excellent assessment of the essential facts and the traditional information, and Marchette Chute, *Shakespeare of London* (New York, 1949; paperback, 1957) stresses Shakespeare's life in the theatre. Two new biographies of Shakespeare have recently appeared. A. L. Rowse, *William Shakespeare: A Biography* (London, 1963; New York, 1964) provides an appraisal by a distinguished English historian, who dismisses the notion that somebody else wrote Shakespeare's plays as arrant nonsense that runs counter to known historical fact. Peter Quennell, *Shakespeare: A Biography* (Cleveland and New York, 1963) is a sensitive and intelligent survey of what is known and surmised of Shakespeare's life. Louis B. Wright, *Shakespeare for Everyman* (paperback; New York, 1964) discusses the basis of Shakespeare's enduring popularity.

The Shakespeare Quarterly, published by the Shakespeare Association of America under the editorship of James G. McManaway, is recommended for those who wish to keep up with current Shakespearean scholarship and stage productions. The

Quarterly includes an annual bibliography of Shakespeare editions and works on Shakespeare published during the previous year.

The question of the authenticity of Shakespeare's plays arouses perennial attention. The theory of hidden cryptograms in the plays is demolished by William F. and Elizebeth S. Friedman, *The Shakespearean Ciphers Examined* (New York, 1957). A succinct account of the various absurdities advanced to suggest the authorship of a multitude of candidates other than Shakespeare will be found in R. C. Churchill, *Shakespeare and His Betters* (Bloomington, Ind., 1959). Another recent discussion of the subject, *The Authorship of Shakespeare*, by James G. McManaway (Washington, D.C., 1962), presents the evidence from contemporary records to prove the identity of Shakespeare the actor-playwright with Shakespeare of Stratford.

Scholars are not in agreement about the details of playhouse construction in the Elizabethan period. John C. Adams presents a plausible reconstruction of the Globe in *The Globe Playhouse: Its Design and Equipment* (Cambridge, Mass., 1942; 2nd rev. ed., 1961). A description with excellent drawings based on Dr. Adams' model is Irwin Smith, *Shakespeare's Globe Playhouse: A Modern Reconstruction in Text and Scale Drawings* (New York, 1956). Other sensible discussions are C. Walter Hodges, *The Globe Restored* (London, 1953) and A. M. Nagler, *Shakespeare's Stage* (New Haven, 1958). Bernard Beckerman, *Shakespeare at the Globe, 1599–1609* (New

Haven, 1962; paperback, 1962) discusses Elizabethan staging and acting techniques.

A sound and readable history of the early theatres is Joseph Quincy Adams, *Shakespearean Playhouses: A History of English Theatres from the Beginnings to the Restoration* (Boston, 1917). For detailed, factual information about the Elizabethan and seventeenth-century stages, the definitive reference works are Sir Edmund Chambers, *The Elizabethan Stage* (4 vols., Oxford, 1923) and Gerald E. Bentley, *The Jacobean and Caroline Stages* (5 vols., Oxford, 1941–1956).

Further information on the history of the theatre and related topics will be found in the following titles: T. W. Baldwin, *The Organization and Personnel of the Shakespearean Company* (Princeton, 1927); Lily Bess Campbell, *Scenes and Machines on the English Stage during the Renaissance* (Cambridge, 1923); Esther Cloudman Dunn, *Shakespeare in America* (New York, 1939); George C. D. Odell, *Shakespeare from Betterton to Irving* (2 vols., London, 1931); Arthur Colby Sprague, *Shakespeare and the Actors: The Stage Business in His Plays (1660–1905)* (Cambridge, Mass., 1944) and *Shakespearian Players and Performances* (Cambridge, Mass., 1953); Leslie Hotson, *The Commonwealth and Restoration Stage* (Cambridge, Mass., 1928); Alwin Thaler, *Shakspere to Sheridan: A Book about the Theatre of Yesterday and To-day* (Cambridge, Mass., 1922); George C. Branam, *Eighteenth-Century Adaptations of Shakespeare's Tragedies* (Berkeley, 1956); C. Beecher Hogan, *Shakespeare in the Theatre, 1701–1800* (Oxford, 1957); Ernest Bradlee Watson, *Sheridan to Robertson: A Study of the 19th-Century London Stage* (Cambridge, Mass., 1926); and Enid Welsford, *The Court Masque* (Cambridge, Mass., 1927).

A brief account of the growth of Shakespeare's reputation is F. E. Halliday, *The Cult of Shakespeare* (London, 1947). A more detailed discussion is given in Augustus Ralli, *A History of Shakespearian Criticism* (2 vols., Oxford, 1932; New York, 1958). Harley Granville-Barker, *Prefaces to Shakespeare* (5 vols., London, 1927–1948; 2 vols., London, 1958) provides stimulating critical discussion of the plays. An older classic of criticism is Andrew C. Bradley, *Shakespearean Tragedy: Lectures on Hamlet, Othello, King Lear, Macbeth* (London, 1904; paperback, 1955). Sir Edmund Chambers, *Shakespeare: A Survey* (London, 1935; paperback, 1958) contains short, sensible essays on thirty-four of the plays, originally written as introductions to single-play editions. Alfred Harbage, *William Shakespeare: A Reader's Guide* (New York, 1963) is a handbook to the reading and appreciation of the plays, with scene synopses and interpretation.

For the history plays see Lily Bess Campbell, *Shakespeare's "Histories": Mirrors of Elizabethan Policy* (Cambridge, 1947); John Palmer, *Political Characters of Shakespeare* (London, 1945; 1961); E. M. W. Tillyard, *Shakespeare's History Plays* (London, 1948); Irving Ribner, *The English History Play in the Age of Shakespeare* (Princeton, 1947);

and Max M. Reese, *The Cease of Majesty* (London, 1961).

The comedies are illuminated by the following studies: C. L. Barber, *Shakespeare's Festive Comedy* (Princeton, 1959); John Russell Brown, *Shakespeare and His Comedies* (London, 1957); H. B. Charlton, *Shakespearian Comedy* (London, 1938; 4th ed., 1949); W. W. Lawrence, *Shakespeare's Problem Comedies* (New York, 1931); and Thomas M. Parrott, *Shakespearean Comedy* (New York, 1949).

Among the special studies that give attention to *The Winter's Tale*, E. M. W. Tillyard, *Shakespeare's Last Plays* (London, 1938) will supply provocative suggestions. A study that attempts to show that Shakespeare had a consistent theological and philosophic purpose in the play is S. L. Bethell, *The Winter's Tale: A Study* (London [1948]). In this connection, see also D. G. James, *Skepticism and Poetry* (London, 1937). Bertrand Evans, *Shakespeare's Comedies* (Oxford, 1960) has a brief section on Shakespeare's dramatic romances. The new Arden text, edited by J. H. P. Pafford (London, 1963) has a meticulous introduction that summarizes recent scholarship on the play.

Further discussions of Shakespeare's tragedies, in addition to Bradley, already cited, are contained in H. B. Charlton, *Shakespearian Tragedy* (Cambridge, 1948); Willard Farnham, *The Medieval Heritage of Elizabethan Tragedy* (Berkeley, 1936) and *Shakespeare's Tragic Frontier: The World of His Final Tragedies* (Berkeley, 1950); and Harold S. Wilson,

On the Design of Shakespearian Tragedy (Toronto, 1957).

The "Roman" plays are treated in M. M. MacCallum, *Shakespeare's Roman Plays and Their Background* (London, 1910) and J. C. Maxwell, "Shakespeare's Roman Plays, 1900–1956," *Shakespeare Survey 10* (Cambridge, 1957), 1-11.

Kenneth Muir, *Shakespeare's Sources: Comedies and Tragedies* (London, 1957) discusses Shakespeare's use of source material. The sources themselves have been reprinted several times. Among old editions are John P. Collier (ed.), *Shakespeare's Library* (2 vols., London, 1850), Israel C. Gollancz (ed.), *The Shakespeare Classics* (12 vols., London, 1907–26), and W. C. Hazlitt (ed.), *Shakespeare's Library* (6 vols., London, 1875). A modern edition is being prepared by Geoffrey Bullough with the title *Narrative and Dramatic Sources of Shakespeare* (London and New York, 1957–). Five volumes, covering the sources for the comedies, histories, and Roman plays, have been published to date (1965).

In addition to the second edition of *Webster's New International Dictionary,* which contains most of the unusual words used by Shakespeare, the following reference works are helpful: Edwin A. Abbott, *A Shakespearian Grammar* (London, 1872); C. T. Onions, *A Shakespeare Glossary* (2nd rev. ed., Oxford, 1925); and Eric Partridge, *Shakespeare's Bawdy* (New York, 1948; paperback, 1960).

Some knowledge of the social background of the period in which Shakespeare lived is important for a full understanding of his work. A brief, clear, and accurate account of Tudor history is S. T. Bindoff, *The Tudors*, in the Penguin series. A readable general history is G. M. Trevelyan, *The History of England*, first published in 1926 and available in numerous editions. The same author's *English Social History*, first published in 1942 and also available in many editions, provides fascinating information about England in all periods. Sir John Neale, *Queen Elizabeth* (London, 1935; paperback, 1957) is the best study of the great Queen. Various aspects of life in the Elizabethan period are treated in Louis B. Wright, *Middle-Class Culture in Elizabethan England* (Chapel Hill, N.C., 1935; reprinted Ithaca, N.Y., 1958, 1964). *Shakespeare's England: An Account of the Life and Manners of His Age*, edited by Sidney Lee and C. T. Onions (2 vols., Oxford, 1917), provides much information on many aspects of Elizabethan life. A fascinating survey of the period will be found in Muriel St. C. Byrne, *Elizabethan Life in Town and Country* (London, 1925; rev. ed., 1954; paperback, 1961).

The Folger Library is issuing a series of illustrated booklets entitled "Folger Booklets on Tudor and Stuart Civilization," printed and distributed by Cornell University Press. Published to date are the following titles:

D. W. Davies, *Dutch Influences on English Culture, 1558–1625*

Giles E. Dawson, *The Life of William Shakespeare*

Ellen C. Eyler, *Early English Gardens and Garden Books*

Elaine W. Fowler, *English Sea Power in the Early Tudor Period, 1485–1558*

John R. Hale, *The Art of War and Renaissance England*

William Haller, *Elizabeth I and the Puritans*

Virginia A. LaMar, *English Dress in the Age of Shakespeare*

_____, *Travel and Roads in England*

John L. Lievsay, *The Elizabethan Image of Italy*

James G. McManaway, *The Authorship of Shakespeare*

Dorothy E. Mason, *Music in Elizabethan England*

Garrett Mattingly, *The "Invincible" Armada and Elizabethan England*

Boies Penrose, *Tudor and Early Stuart Voyaging*

Conyers Read, *The Government of England under Elizabeth*

T. I. Rae, *Scotland in the Time of Shakespeare*

Albert J. Schmidt, *The Yeoman in Tudor and Stuart England*

Lilly C. Stone, *English Sports and Recreations*

Craig R. Thompson, *The Bible in English, 1525–1611*

_____, *The English Church in the Sixteenth Century*

_____, *Schools in Tudor England*

_____, *Universities in Tudor England*

Louis B. Wright, *Shakespeare's Theatre and the Dramatic Tradition*

At intervals the Folger Library plans to gather these booklets in hardbound volumes. The first is *Life and Letters in Tudor and Stuart England, First Folger Series,* edited by Louis B. Wright and Virginia A. LaMar (published for the Folger Shakespeare Library by Cornell University Press, 1962). The volume contains eleven of the separate booklets.

The Names of the Actors

Leontes, King of Sicilia.

Mamillius, young Prince of Sicilia.

Camillo,
Antigonus,
Cleomenes,
Dion,
} four Lords of Sicilia.

Polixenes, King of Bohemia.

Florizel, Prince of Bohemia.

Archidamus, a Lord of Bohemia.

Old Shepherd, reputed father of *Perdita*.

Clown, his son.

Autolycus, a rogue.

[*A Mariner.*]

[*A Jailer.*]

Hermione, queen to *Leontes*.

Perdita, daughter to *Leontes* and *Hermione*.

Paulina, wife to *Antigonus*.

Emilia, a lady [attending on *Hermione*].

[*Mopsa*,
[*Dorcas*,
} *Shepherdesses*.]

Other Lords, Gentlemen, and Servants; Shepherds and Shepherdesses; [Time as Chorus].

[SCENE: *Sicilia and Bohemia.*]

THE
WINTER'S
TALE

ACT I

I.i. The Sicilian Lord Camillo and Archidamus, a Lord of Bohemia, discuss the current visit to King Leontes of his old friend, the King of Bohemia. The two Kings were educated together as children; although they have been separated for many years, the visit of the King of Bohemia has confirmed their mutual affection.

<hr/>

3. **on foot:** undertaken (the service being attendance on his sovereign).

8-9. **Wherein our entertainment shall shame us, we will be justified in our loves:** we will make up in affection for any defect in the quality of entertainment we offer.

11-2. **in the freedom of my knowledge:** with the frankness that my knowledge warrants.

13-4. **sleepy drinks:** drinks inducing sleep.

14-5. **insufficience:** deficiency.

17. **You pay a great deal too dear:** you offer excessive thanks.

ACT I

Scene I. [Sicilia. Antechamber in Leontes' palace.]

Enter Camillo and Archidamus.

Arch. If you shall chance, Camillo, to visit Bohemia, on the like occasion whereon my services are now on foot, you shall see, as I have said, great difference betwixt our Bohemia and your Sicilia.

Cam. I think, this coming summer, the King of   5
Sicilia means to pay Bohemia the visitation which he justly owes him.

Arch. Wherein our entertainment shall shame us, we will be justified in our loves; for indeed—

Cam. Beseech you—   10

Arch. Verily, I speak it in the freedom of my knowledge. We cannot with such magnificence—in so rare—I know not what to say. We will give you sleepy drinks, that your senses, unintelligent of our insufficience, may, though they cannot praise us, as little   15
accuse us.

Cam. You pay a great deal too dear for what's given freely.

Arch. Believe me, I speak as my understanding instructs me and as mine honesty puts it to utterance.   20

I

27. **attorneyed:** carried on by agents.
29. **that:** so that.
30. **vast:** empty expanse; chasm.
35. **of:** from.
36. **into my note:** under my notice.
38-9. **physics the subject:** comforts the nation (all the King's subjects).

2

Cam. Sicilia cannot show himself overkind to Bohemia. They were trained together in their childhoods; and there rooted betwixt them then such an affection, which cannot choose but branch now. Since their more mature dignities and royal necessities 25 made separation of their society, their encounters, though not personal, have been royally attorneyed with interchange of gifts, letters, loving embassies; that they have seemed to be together, though absent; shook hands, as over a vast; and embraced, as it were, 30 from the ends of opposed winds. The Heavens continue their loves!

Arch. I think there is not in the world either malice or matter to alter it. You have an unspeakable comfort of your young Prince Mamillius. It is a gentleman of 35 the greatest promise that ever came into my note.

Cam. I very well agree with you in the hopes of him. It is a gallant child; one that indeed physics the subject, makes old hearts fresh. They that went on crutches ere he was born desire yet their life to see 40 him a man.

Arch. Would they else be content to die?

Cam. Yes; if there were no other excuse why they should desire to live.

Arch. If the King had no son, they would desire to 45 live on crutches till he had one.

Exeunt.

I.ii. Polixenes, anxious to return to Bohemia, is finally persuaded by Leontes' wife, Hermione, to stay another week. Leontes is suddenly seized with unreasonable jealousy of his friend. Hermione and Polixenes notice that he is disturbed but do not guess the reason. When they stroll away to the garden, Leontes voices his suspicions to Camillo, who tries unsuccessfully to convince him of his mistake. Leontes insists that the guilty pair are plotting his murder and orders Camillo to forestall them by killing Polixenes. At the first opportunity Camillo warns Polixenes of the King's delusion and urges him to fly. Since his disobedience of Leontes' order places his own life in danger, Camillo decides to accompany Polixenes to Bohemia.

1. **wat'ry star:** moon (which was believed to control all watery things).

2. **The shepherd's note:** i.e., the shepherd has observed the lapse of nine months.

4. **Would:** should.

6-9. **like a cipher,/ Yet standing in rich place, I multiply/ With one "We thank you" many thousands mo/ That go before it:** like a zero, so placed as to enlarge the value of the figure, my single thank you must stand for many. **Mo** (not a form of "more") means "many additional."

11. **part:** depart.

13-6. **I am . . . truly":** I am anxious lest my absence may result in troubles at home that will justify my utmost fears. This elliptical passage is difficult and cannot be analyzed grammatically. **Sneaping** means "nipping," the image suggesting plants being spoiled by a frosty wind.

3

(Continued on next page)

Scene II. [A room of state in Leontes' palace.]

Enter Leontes, Hermione, Mamillius, Polixenes, Camillo, [and Attendants].

Pol. Nine changes of the wat'ry star hath been
The shepherd's note since we have left our throne
Without a burden: time as long again
Would be filled up, my brother, with our thanks;
And yet we should, for perpetuity,   5
Go hence in debt: and therefore, like a cipher,
Yet standing in rich place, I multiply
With one "We thank you" many thousands mo
That go before it.
Leon.   Stay your thanks a while,   10
And pay them when you part.
Pol.   Sir, that's tomorrow.
I am questioned by my fears of what may chance
Or breed upon our absence, that may blow
No sneaping winds at home, to make us say,   15
"This is put forth too truly": besides, I have stayed
To tire your royalty.
Leon.   We are tougher, brother,
Than you can put us to't.
Pol.   No longer stay.   20
Leon. One sennight longer.
Pol.   Very sooth, tomorrow.
Leon. We'll part the time between's, then: and in that
I'll no gainsaying.   25

18-9. **We are tougher . . . / Than you can put us to't:** my strength exceeds your power to tire it.

22. **Very sooth:** indeed.

23. **part:** divide equally.

25. **gainsaying:** denial.

32-3. **which to hinder/ Were in your love a whip to me:** the hindering of my departure, although it was caused by your affection, would be painful to me.

42. **The bygone day proclaimed:** was announced in news received yesterday; **Say:** if you say.

43. **He's beat from his best ward:** you deprive him of his best excuse. The phrase is from fencing.

45. **were:** would be.

46. **But:** merely.

48. **distaffs:** symbolizing women. To Hermione, a mother herself, Polixenes' desire to see his child would be an unanswerable excuse for departure.

49. **adventure:** risk.

51. **commission:** allowance; permission.

52. **let him:** delay himself; tarry; **gest:** period allotted for staying.

53. **Prefixed:** predetermined; **good deed:** truly.

54. **jar:** tick; i.e., not a bit less.

55. **What lady she her lord:** any lady (loves) her husband.

Pol.   Press me not, beseech you, so.
There is no tongue that moves, none, none i' the
     world,
So soon as yours could win me. So it should now,
Were there necessity in your request, although   30
'Twere needful I denied it. My affairs
Do even drag me homeward: which to hinder
Were in your love a whip to me; my stay
To you a charge and trouble. To save both,
Farewell, our brother.   35

Leon.   Tongue-tied, our queen? Speak
     you.

Her. I had thought, sir, to have held my peace until
You had drawn oaths from him not to stay. You, sir,
Charge him too coldly. Tell him, you are sure   40
All in Bohemia's well; this satisfaction
The bygone day proclaimed. Say this to him,
He's beat from his best ward.

Leon.   Well said, Hermione.

Her. To tell he longs to see his son were strong: 45
But let him say so then, and let him go;
But let him swear so, and he shall not stay,
We'll thwack him hence with distaffs.
[*To Polixenes*]
Yet of your royal presence I'll adventure
The borrow of a week. When at Bohemia   50
You take my lord, I'll give him my commission
To let him there a month behind the gest
Prefixed for's parting: yet, good deed, Leontes,
I love thee not a jar o' the clock behind
What lady she her lord. You'll stay?   55

60. **limber:** limp; weak.

61. **unsphere:** i.e., move from their spheres.

67. **fees:** Elizabethan prisoners were not kept at state expense but had to pay fees for their food and board while in prison.

73. **import:** imply.

79. **lordings:** little gentlemen.

81. **behind:** to come; in the future.

Pol.   No, madam.
Her. Nay, but you will?
Pol.   I may not, verily.
Her. Verily!
You put me off with limber vows; but I,   60
Though you would seek t'unsphere the stars with
    oaths,
Should yet say, "Sir, no going." Verily,
You shall not go: a lady's "Verily"'s
As potent as a lord's. Will you go yet?   65
Force me to keep you as a prisoner,
Not like a guest: so you shall pay your fees
When you depart, and save your thanks. How say
    you?
My prisoner? or my guest? By your dread "Verily,"   70
One of them you shall be.
Pol.   Your guest, then, madam:
To be your prisoner should import offending;
Which is for me less easy to commit
Than you to punish.   75
Her.   Not your jailer, then,
But your kind hostess. Come, I'll question you
Of my lord's tricks and yours when you were boys.
You were pretty lordings then?
Pol.   We were, fair queen,   80
Two lads that thought there was no more behind
But such a day tomorrow as today,
And to be boy eternal.
Her.   Was not my lord
The verier wag o' the two?   85

88. **changed:** exchanged.

93. **blood:** affections, such as passion.

95-6. **the imposition cleared/ Hereditary ours:** being cleared of our inheritance of original sin.

104. **Grace to boot:** Heaven help us!

Pol. We were as twinned lambs that did frisk i' the
    sun,
And bleat the one at the other. What we changed
Was innocence for innocence; we knew not
The doctrine of ill-doing, nor dreamed   90
That any did. Had we pursued that life,
And our weak spirits ne'er been higher reared
With stronger blood, we should have answered
    Heaven
Boldly, "Not guilty"; the imposition cleared   95
Hereditary ours.
    Her.   By this we gather
You have tripped since.
    Pol.   O my most sacred lady!
Temptations have since then been born to's: for   100
In those unfledged days was my wife a girl;
Your precious self had then not crossed the eyes
Of my young playfellow.
    Her.   Grace to boot!
Of this make no conclusion, lest you say   105
Your queen and I are devils. Yet go on;
The offenses we have made you do we'll answer,
If you first sinned with us, and that with us
You did continue fault, and that you slipped not
With any but with us.   110
    Leon.   Is he won yet?
    Her. He'll stay, my lord.
    Leon.   At my request he would not.
Hermione, my dearest, thou never spokest
To better purpose.   115
    Her.   Never?

121-22. **tongueless:** without having been tongued (praised).

123. **waiting:** dependent.

124-26. **you may ride's/ With one soft kiss a thousand furlongs ere/ With spur we heat an acre:** i.e., just as with horses, you may handle us women better with affection than with punishment; we will carry you faster on one kiss than we can be urged with a taste of the spur. **Heat** means "race at top speed."

129. **would her name were Grace:** would that the deed were gracious (holy).

133. **crabbed:** vexatious; trying.

136. **clap:** pledge, with a handclasp.

138. **'Tis Grace indeed:** referring to the proverbial saying that "Marriages are made in Heaven." Her word savored of divinity because it led to their marriage.

143. **far:** the old comparative, "farther"; **mingling bloods:** growing intimate.

144. **tremor cordis:** a heart flutter.

145-48. **This entertainment/ May a free face put on, derive a liberty/ From heartiness, from bounty, fertile bosom,/ And well become the agent:** Hermione's warmth of manner may derive from the sincerity and generosity of her nature, which would do her credit.

  Leon.   Never, but once.
  Her. What! Have I twice said well? When was't
   before?
I prithee tell me: cram's with praise, and make's   120
As fat as tame things. One good deed dying tongue-
   less
Slaughters a thousand waiting upon that.
Our praises are our wages: you may ride's
With one soft kiss a thousand furlongs ere   125
With spur we heat an acre. But to the goal.
My last good deed was to entreat his stay:
What was my first? It has an elder sister,
Or I mistake you. Oh, would her name were Grace!
But once before I spoke to the purpose. When?   130
Nay, let me have't: I long.
  Leon.   Why, that was when
Three crabbed months had soured themselves to
   death
Ere I could make thee open thy white hand   135
And clap thyself my love: then didst thou utter,
"I am yours forever."
  Her.   'Tis Grace indeed.
Why, lo you now, I have spoke to the purpose twice:
The one forever earned a royal husband,   140
The other for some while a friend.
         [Takes Polixenes' hand]
  Leon. [*Aside*]   Too hot, too hot!
To mingle friendship far is mingling bloods.
I have *tremor cordis* on me: my heart dances,
But not for joy; not joy. This entertainment   145
May a free face put on, derive a liberty

152. **The mort o' the deer:** Shakespeare may have remembered a common emblem of a mortally wounded deer that symbolized incurable love. See cut, p. 9. **Mort** means death.

153. **brows:** Leontes thinks of the horns that were figuratively said to sprout from the forehead of a man whose wife had betrayed him.

156. **I' fecks:** in faith; truly.

157. **bawcock:** fine fellow (a corruption of French *beau coq*).

161. **steer . . . heifer . . . calf:** all horned animals.

162. **virginalling:** strumming; paddling.

163. **wanton:** playful.

166. **wantst:** lack; **rough pash:** shaggy head; **shoots:** budding horns.

168. **full:** completely.

170-71. **false/ As o'erdyed blacks:** unstable, like the color of a black garment overdyed with another color, or, perhaps, redyed too often.

173. **bourn:** boundary.

175. **welkin:** sky blue.

176. **Most dear'st! my collop!:** probably an allusion to a proverb "It is a dear collop [morsel] that is taken out of the flesh"; **dam:** mother.

177-85. **Affection . . . brows:** lustful inclination! thy intensity pierces the very heart. You make possible things formerly held incredible, deal in fantasy, . . . work together with imaginary things, and are intimate with incorporeality. Then 'tis very credible that you can couple with reality; and (in this instance) you do, entirely unlawfully, and I know it,

8

From heartiness, from bounty, fertile bosom,
And well become the agent; 't may, I grant;
But to be paddling palms and pinching fingers,
As now they are, and making practiced smiles,   150
As in a looking glass, and then to sigh, as 'twere
The mort o' the deer—oh, that is entertainment
My bosom likes not, nor my brows! Mamillius,
Art thou my boy?
    Mam.   Ay, my good lord.   155
    Leon.   I' fecks!
Why, that's my bawcock. What, hast smutched thy
    nose?
They say it is a copy out of mine. Come, captain,
We must be neat; not neat, but cleanly, captain: 160
And yet the steer, the heifer, and the calf
Are all called neat.—Still virginalling
Upon his palm!—How now, you wanton calf!
Art thou my calf?
    Mam.   Yes, if you will, my lord.   165
    Leon. Thou wantst a rough pash and the shoots
    that I have,
To be full like me: yet they say we are
Almost as like as eggs; women say so,
That will say anything. But were they false   170
As o'erdyed blacks, as wind, as waters, false
As dice are to be wished by one that fixes
No bourn 'twixt his and mine, yet were it true
To say this boy were like me. Come, sir page,
Look on me with your welkin eye. Sweet villain!   175
Most dear'st! my collop! Can thy dam?—may't be?—
Affection! thy intention stabs the center:

so that my mind is distracted and I feel my horns sprouting.

187. **something seems:** seems somewhat.

192. **moved:** distressed; angry.

193. **in good earnest:** truthfully.

195. **pastime:** source of amusement.

198-99. **unbreeched,/ In my green velvet coat:** boys were dressed in gowns until about the age of six.

203. **squash:** green peapod; hence, youth.

204. **take eggs for money:** a proverbial saying meaning to be content with a bad bargain.

206. **happy man be's dole:** proverbial: "good luck to you."

The wounded stag, symbolizing incurable love. From Gabriele Simeoni, *Le sententiose imprese* (1560). (See I.ii. 152.)

Thou dost make possible things not so held,
Communicatest with dreams—how can this be?—
With what's unreal thou coactive art,   180
And fellowst nothing. Then 'tis very credent
Thou mayst co-join with something; and thou dost,
And that beyond commission, and I find it,
And that to the infection of my brains
And hard'ning of my brows.   185
   Pol.   What means Sicilia?
   Her. He something seems unsettled.
   Pol.   How, my lord!
What cheer? How is't with you, best brother?
   Her.   You look 190
As if you held a brow of much distraction.
Are you moved, my lord?
   Leon.   No, in good earnest.
How sometimes nature will betray its folly,
Its tenderness, and make itself a pastime   195
To harder bosoms! Looking on the lines
Of my boy's face, methoughts I did recoil
Twenty-three years and saw myself unbreeched,
In my green velvet coat, my dagger muzzled,
Lest it should bite its master and so prove,   200
As ornaments oft do, too dangerous.
How like, methought, I then was to this kernel,
This squash, this gentleman. Mine honest friend,
Will you take eggs for money?
   Mam. No, my lord, I'll fight.   205
   Leon. You will! Why, happy man be's dole! My
    brother,

211. **exercise:** occupation; **matter:** concern.

213. **parasite:** dependant.

215. **varying childness:** childish caprices.

216. **thick my blood:** cause melancholy.

217-18. **So stands this squire / Officed with me:** this lad performs the same service for me.

223. **Apparent:** heir apparent; possessor.

225. **Shall's attend you:** shall we await you.

226. **bents:** inclinations.

229. **give line:** play you, like a fisherman with a fish.

230. **Go to:** come, come (expressing disapproval of what he thinks he sees).

233. **allowing:** conferring the right; i.e., if he were her husband, such behavior would be perfectly proper.

235-36. **forked one:** horned one; cuckold.

Are you so fond of your young prince as we
Do seem to be of ours?
   Pol.   If at home, sir,   210
He's all my exercise, my mirth, my matter:
Now my sworn friend, and then mine enemy;
My parasite, my soldier, statesman, all.
He makes a July's day short as December;
And with his varying childness cures in me   215
Thoughts that would thick my blood.
   Leon.   So stands this squire
Officed with me. We two will walk, my lord,
And leave you to your graver steps. Hermione,
How thou lovest us, show in our brother's welcome; 220
Let what is dear in Sicily be cheap.
Next to thyself and my young rover, he's
Apparent to my heart.
   Her.   If you would seek us,
We are yours i' the garden. Shall's attend you there? 225
   Leon. To your own bents dispose you: you'll be
      found,
Be you beneath the sky. [*Aside*] I am angling now,
Though you perceive me not how I give line.
Go to, go to!   230
How she holds up the neb, the bill to him!
And arms her with the boldness of a wife
To her allowing husband!
    [*Exeunt Polixenes, Hermione, and Attendants.*]
                      Gone already!
Inch-thick, knee-deep, o'er head and ears a forked 235
    one!
Go, play, boy, play: thy mother plays, and I

238. **issue:** outcome.

247. **there's comfort in't:** cf. the proverb "Misery loves company."

250. **revolted:** unfaithful.

251. **Physic:** remedy.

252-53. **that will strike/ Where 'tis predominant:** and its influence causes bawdy behavior to be widespread.

254. **Be it concluded:** the conclusion must be accepted.

257. **on's:** of us.

266. **still:** always.

Play too; but so disgraced a part, whose issue
Will hiss me to my grave. Contempt and clamor
Will be my knell. Go, play, boy, play. There have 240
    been,
Or I am much deceived, cuckolds ere now;
And many a man there is, even at this present,
Now, while I speak this, holds his wife by the arm,
That little thinks she has been sluiced in's absence 245
And his pond fished by his next neighbor, by
Sir Smile, his neighbor. Nay, there's comfort in't
Whiles other men have gates and those gates opened,
As mine, against their will. Should all despair
That have revolted wives, the tenth of mankind 250
Would hang themselves. Physic for't there's none:
It is a bawdy planet, that will strike
Where 'tis predominant; and 'tis pow'rful, think it,
From east, west, north, and south. Be it concluded,
No barricado for a belly! Know't: 255
It will let in and out the enemy
With bag and baggage. Many thousand on's
Have the disease and feel't not. How now, boy!
    Mam. I am like you, they say.
    Leon.   Why, that's some comfort. 260
What, Camillo there?
    Cam. Ay, my good lord.
    Leon. Go play, Mamillius; thou'rt an honest man.
                              [*Exit Mamillius.*]
Camillo, this great sir will yet stay longer.
    Cam. You had much ado to make his anchor hold; 265
When you cast out, it still came home.
    Leon.   Didst note it?

269. **material:** important.

271. **They're here with me already:** they have already noticed my shame.

272. **rounding:** whispering insinuations.

274. **When I shall gust it last:** since I would be the last to sense it, referring to the proverb "The cuckold is the last that knows of it."

279. **so it is:** as the situation stands; **taken:** understood.

281. **conceit:** power of thought; **soaking:** capable of ready absorption.

282. **blocks:** blockheads.

283. **severals:** individuals.

284. **Lower messes:** baser groups. A mess was a group of four, the usual subdivision of a large dinner party.

285. **purblind:** totally blind.

287. **Bohemia:** the King of Bohemia.

297. **chamber counsels:** private confidences.

Cam. He would not stay at your petitions, made
His business more material.

Leon.   Didst perceive it?   270
[*Aside*] They're here with me already; whisp'ring,
   rounding,
"Sicilia is a so-forth." 'Tis far gone
When I shall gust it last.—How came't, Camillo,
That he did stay?   275

Cam.   At the good Queen's entreaty.

Leon. At the Queen's be't: "good" should be
   pertinent;
But, so it is, it is not. Was this taken
By any understanding pate but thine?   280
For thy conceit is soaking, will draw in
More than the common blocks: not noted, is't,
But of the finer natures? By some severals
Of headpiece extraordinary? Lower messes
Perchance are to this business purblind? Say.   285

Cam. Business, my lord! I think most understand
Bohemia stays here longer.

Leon.   Ha!

Cam.   Stays here longer.

Leon. Ay, but why?   290

Cam. To satisfy your Highness and the entreaties
Of our most gracious mistress.

Leon.   Satisfy!
The entreaties of your mistress! Satisfy!
Let that suffice. I have trusted thee, Camillo,   295
With all the nearest things to my heart, as well
My chamber counsels; wherein, priest-like, thou
Hast cleansed my bosom, I from thee departed

303. **bide:** dwell; linger.
305. **hoxes:** hamstrings.
307. **grafted in:** artificially attached to.
309. **home:** to the finish.
317. **puts forth:** shows itself.
323. **execution:** necessity of performance.
326. **allowed:** tolerated.

Thy penitent reformed: but we have been
Deceived in thy integrity, deceived   300
In that which seems so.

   Cam.   Be it forbid, my lord!

   Leon. To bide upon't, thou art not honest; or,
If thou inclinest that way, thou art a coward,
Which hoxes honesty behind, restraining   305
From course required; or else thou must be counted
A servant grafted in my serious trust
And therein negligent; or else a fool
That seest a game played home, the rich stake
     drawn,   310
And takest it all for jest.

   Cam.   My gracious lord,
I may be negligent, foolish, and fearful;
In every one of these no man is free
But that his negligence, his folly, fear,   315
Among the infinite doings of the world,
Sometime puts forth. In your affairs, my lord,
If ever I were willful-negligent,
It was my folly; if industriously
I played the fool, it was my negligence,   320
Not weighing well the end; if ever fearful
To do a thing, where I the issue doubted,
Whereof the execution did cry out
Against the non-performance, 'twas a fear
Which oft infects the wisest. These, my lord,   325
Are such allowed infirmities that honesty
Is never free of. But, beseech your Grace,
Be plainer with me; let me know my trespass

334. **vision:** spectacle.

337. **slippery:** dishonest; unchaste.

340. **hobbyhorse:** wanton.

345. **present:** immediate; **'Shrew:** beshrew; plague take.

351. **career:** course, literally a horse's gallop.

356. **the pin and web:** cataracts.

By its own visage. If I then deny it,
'Tis none of mine.   330
    Leon.   Ha' not you seen, Camillo—
But that's past doubt, you have, or your eyeglass
Is thicker than a cuckold's horn—or heard—
For to a vision so apparent rumor
Cannot be mute—or thought—for cogitation   335
Resides not in that man that does not think—
My wife is slippery? If thou wilt confess,
Or else be impudently negative,
To have nor eyes nor ears nor thought, then say
My wife's a hobbyhorse; deserves a name   340
As rank as any flax wench that puts to
Before her trothplight: say't and justify't.
    Cam. I would not be a stander-by to hear
My sovereign mistress clouded so, without
My present vengeance taken. 'Shrew my heart,   345
You never spoke what did become you less
Than this; which to reiterate were sin
As deep as that, though true.
    Leon.   Is whispering nothing?
Is leaning cheek to cheek? is meeting noses?   350
Kissing with inside lip? stopping the career
Of laughter with a sigh?—a note infallible
Of breaking honesty—horsing foot on foot?
Skulking in corners? wishing clocks more swift?
Hours, minutes? noon, midnight? and all eyes   355
Blind with the pin and web but theirs, theirs only,
That would unseen be wicked? Is this nothing?
Why, then the world and all that's in't is nothing;
The covering sky is nothing; Bohemia nothing;

364. **betimes:** promptly.
382. **particular thrifts:** personal gains.
383. **undo:** ruin; prevent; **doing:** sexual activity.
384. **form:** seat.
385. **benched:** given a place of greater honor;
worship: dignity.
387. **galled:** injured.
388. **lasting wink:** everlasting sleep.
389. **were:** would be; **cordial:** restorative.

My wife is nothing; nor nothing have these noth-   360
    ings,
If this be nothing.
   Cam.   Good my lord, be cured
Of this diseased opinion, and betimes;
For 'tis most dangerous.   365
   Leon.   Say it be, 'tis true.
   Cam. No, no, my lord.
   Leon.   It is! You lie, you lie!
I say thou liest, Camillo, and I hate thee,
Pronounce thee a gross lout, a mindless slave,   370
Or else a hovering temporizer, that
Canst with thine eyes at once see good and evil,
Inclining to them both. Were my wife's liver
Infected as her life, she would not live
The running of one glass.   375
   Cam.   Who does infect her?
   Leon. Why, he that wears her like her medal, hang-
    ing
About his neck, Bohemia: who, if I
Had servants true about me that bare eyes   380
To see alike mine honor as their profits,
Their own particular thrifts, they would do that
Which should undo more doing. Ay, and thou,
His cupbearer—whom I from meaner form
Have benched and reared to worship, who mayst see   385
Plainly as Heaven sees earth and earth sees Heaven,
How I am galled—mightst bespice a cup
To give mine enemy a lasting wink;
Which draught to me were cordial.
   Cam.   Sir, my lord,   390

393. **Maliciously:** violently (so as to cause poison to be suspected).

394. **crack:** defect.

395. **sovereignly:** surpassingly.

397. **Make that thy question:** i.e., if you are going to question (that Hermione is guilty).

399. **appoint myself in this vexation:** choose to be distressed in this way.

405. **ripe moving to't:** the motivation of sound judgment.

406. **blench:** go astray; swerve in judgment.

408. **fetch off:** take care of; but the phrase also meant "rescue," which is what Camillo proceeds to do. The ambiguity is probably deliberate.

411-12. **forsealing/ The injury of tongues:** tightly sealing up tongues that might utter slander.

418. **clear:** innocent.

I could do this, and that with no rash potion
But with a ling'ring dram that should not work
Maliciously like poison; but I cannot
Believe this crack to be in my dread mistress,
So sovereignly being honorable.   395
I have loved thee—

   Leon.   Make that thy question and go rot!
Dost think I am so muddy, so unsettled,
To appoint myself in this vexation; sully
The purity and whiteness of my sheets,   400
Which to preserve is sleep, which being spotted
Is goads, thorns, nettles, tails of wasps;
Give scandal to the blood o' the Prince my son,
Who I do think is mine and love as mine,
Without ripe moving to't? Would I do this?   405
Could man so blench?

   Cam.   I must believe you, sir.
I do; and will fetch off Bohemia for't;
Provided that, when he's removed, your Highness
Will take again your queen as yours at first,   410
Even for your son's sake; and thereby forsealing
The injury of tongues in courts and kingdoms
Known and allied to yours.

   Leon.   Thou dost advise me
Even so as I mine own course have set down: 415
I'll give no blemish to her honor, none.

   Cam. My lord,
Go then; and with a countenance as clear
As friendship wears at feasts, keep with Bohemia
And with your queen. I am his cupbearer: 420

423. **This is all:** this is what the matter comes to.
429. **for:** as for.
431. **ground:** reason.
433. **in rebellion with himself:** acting contrary to his own nature.

If from me he have wholesome beverage,
Account me not your servant.
  Leon.   This is all:
Do't, and thou hast the one half of my heart;
Do't not, thou splittst thine own.   425
  Cam.   I'll do't, my lord.
  Leon. I will seem friendly, as thou hast advised
    me.   *Exit.*
  Cam. O miserable lady! But, for me,
What case stand I in? I must be the poisoner   430
Of good Polixenes; and my ground to do't
Is the obedience to a master, one
Who, in rebellion with himself, will have
All that are his so too. To do this deed,
Promotion follows. If I could find example   435
Of thousands that had struck anointed kings
And flourished after, I'd not do't; but since
Nor brass nor stone nor parchment bears not one,
Let villainy itself forswear't. I must
Forsake the court. To do't, or no, is certain   440
To me a breakneck. Happy star reign now!
Here comes Bohemia.

Enter Polixenes.

  Pol.   This is strange: methinks
My favor here begins to warp. Not speak?
Good day, Camillo.   445
  Cam.   Hail, most royal sir!
  Pol. What is the news i' the court?
  Cam.   None rare, my lord.

450. **As:** as if.

452. **compliment:** courtesy.

453. **falling:** dropping.

455. **what is breeding:** in modern terms, "what's up."

460. **intelligent:** informative; **'tis thereabouts:** that's where the trouble is: I dare know but do not know.

463-64. **Your changed complexions are to me a mirror/ Which shows me mine changed too:** your changes of expression show me how anxiety must have altered my own.

472. **sighted like the basilisk:** equipped like the legendary basilisk with a deadly glance.

473. **sped:** prospered.

475. **thereto:** in addition.

476. **Clerklike experienced:** well-educated.

477. **gentry:** gentle birth.

478. **In whose success we are gentle:** from whom we derive our gentility.

Pol. The King hath on him such a countenance
As he had lost some province, and a region   450
Loved as he loves himself. Even now I met him
With customary compliment; when he,
Wafting his eyes to the contrary, and falling
A lip of much contempt, speeds from me and
So leaves me, to consider what is breeding   455
That changes thus his manners.
   Cam. I dare not know, my lord.
   Pol. How! dare not! do not! Do you know, and
     dare not?
Be intelligent to me: 'tis thereabouts;   460
For, to yourself, what you do know, you must,
And cannot say you dare not. Good Camillo,
Your changed complexions **are** to me a mirror
Which shows me mine changed too; for I must be
A party in this alteration, finding   465
Myself thus altered with't.
   Cam.   There is a sickness
Which puts some of us in distemper, but
I cannot name the disease; and it is caught
Of you that yet are well.   470
   Pol.   How! caught of me!
Make me not sighted like the basilisk.
I have looked on thousands who have sped the better
By my regard, but killed none so. Camillo—
As you are certainly a gentleman; thereto   475
Clerklike experienced, which no less adorns
Our gentry than our parents' noble names,
In whose success we are gentle—I beseech you,

479-81. **which does behoove my knowledge/ Thereof to be informed:** which it is necessary for me to know.

482. **ignorant concealment:** concealment that leaves Polixenes ignorant.

486. **conjure:** implore.

486-87. **all the parts of man/ Which honor does acknowledge:** all the things men account honorable.

489-90. **What incidency thou dost guess of harm/ Is creeping toward me:** what harm you suspect is likely to come upon me.

500. **appointed him to murder you:** selected as the man who is to murder you.

505. **As:** as if.

506. **vice:** press.

If you know aught which does behoove my knowl-
    edge   480
Thereof to be informed, imprison't not
In ignorant concealment.
    Cam.   I may not answer.
    Pol. A sickness caught of me, and yet I well!
I must be answered. Dost thou hear, Camillo?   485
I conjure thee, by all the parts of man
Which honor does acknowledge, whereof the least
Is not this suit of mine, that thou declare
What incidency thou dost guess of harm
Is creeping toward me; how far off, how near;   490
Which way to be prevented, if to be;
If not, how best to bear it.
    Cam.   Sir, I will tell you,
Since I am charged in honor and by him
That I think honorable: therefore mark my counsel, 495
Which must be ev'n as swiftly followed as
I mean to utter it, or both yourself and me
Cry lost, and so good night!
    Pol.   On, good Camillo.
    Cam. I am appointed him to murder you.   500
    Pol. By whom, Camillo?
    Cam.   By the King.
    Pol.   For what?
    Cam. He thinks, nay, with all confidence he swears,
As he had seen't, or been an instrument   505
To vice you to't, that you have touched his queen
Forbiddenly.
    Pol.   Oh, then, my best blood turn
To an infected jelly, and my name

510. **the Best:** Jesus, referring to Judas' betrayal.

516. **Swear his thought over:** i.e., if you should outswear (deny) his accusation.

520. **or . . . or:** either . . . or.

524. **How should this grow:** how could this suspicion develop.

528. **trunk:** body.

530. **whisper:** summon secretly.

531. **posterns:** gates.

534. **this discovery:** this revelation (of Leontes' plot).

536. **prove:** test.

Be yoked with his that did betray the Best!   510
Turn then my freshest reputation to
A savor that may strike the dullest nostril
Where I arrive, and my approach be shunned,
Nay, hated too, worse than the great'st infection
That e'er was heard or read!   515
   Cam.   Swear his thought over
By each particular star in Heaven and
By all their influences, you may as well
Forbid the sea for to obey the moon,
As or by oath remove or counsel shake   520
The fabric of his folly, whose foundation
Is piled upon his faith and will continue
The standing of his body.
   Pol.   How should this grow?
   Cam. I know not: but I am sure 'tis safer to   525
Avoid what's grown than question how 'tis born.
If therefore you dare trust my honesty,
That lies enclosed in this trunk which you
Shall bear along impawned, away tonight!
Your followers I will whisper to the business;   530
And will by twos and threes, at several posterns,
Clear them o' the city. For myself, I'll put
My fortunes to your service, which are here
By this discovery lost. Be not uncertain;
For, by the honor of my parents, I   535
Have uttered truth: which if you seek to prove,
I dare not stand by; nor shall you be safer
Than one condemned by the King's own mouth, there-
     on
His execution sworn.   540

543-44. thy places shall/ Still neighbor mine: thou shalt ever be at my side in a place of honor.

551. Professed: professed friendship.

553. expedition: speedy departure.

554-55. part of his theme but nothing/ Of his ill-ta'en suspicion: included in the King's displeasure but innocent of what he suspects.

556. respect: regard.

557. avoid: be gone.

Pol.   I do believe thee:
I saw his heart in 's face. Give me thy hand.
Be pilot to me and thy places shall
Still neighbor mine. My ships are ready, and
My people did expect my hence departure   545
Two days ago. This jealousy
Is for a precious creature: as she's rare,
Must it be great; and, as his person's mighty,
Must it be violent; and as he does conceive
He is dishonored by a man which ever   550
Professed to him, why, his revenges must
In that be made more bitter. Fear o'ershades me:
Good expedition be my friend and comfort
The gracious Queen, part of his theme but nothing
Of his ill-ta'en suspicion! Come, Camillo;   555
I will respect thee as a father if
Thou bearst my life off hence. Let us avoid.
    Cam. It is in mine authority to command
The keys of all the posterns. Please your Highness
To take the urgent hour. Come, sir, away.   560
                                        Exeunt.

THE WINTER'S TALE

ACT II

II.i. Hermione is playing with her young son, Mamillius, when Leontes enters and announces Polixenes' flight with Camillo. He orders Mamillius taken from his mother and charges that Polixenes fathered the child she is carrying. Officers escort Hermione and her ladies to prison. Antigonus and another lord try to convince Leontes that he is mistaken, but the King will not see reason: Camillo's treachery has confirmed his suspicions. He announces that he has sent Cleomenes and Dion to consult Apollo's oracle to determine the question of Hermione's guilt. In the meantime, he fears that, if allowed her freedom, she may murder him.

॥॥॥॥॥॥॥॥॥॥॥॥॥॥॥॥॥॥॥॥॥॥॥॥॥॥

1. **he so troubles me:** Hermione is playful rather than serious.

15. **taught 'this:** taught (you) this.

ACT II

Scene I. [A room in Leontes' palace.]

Enter Hermione, Mamillius, [and] Ladies.

Her. Take the boy to you: he so troubles me,
'Tis past enduring.
1. La.   Come, my gracious lord,
Shall I be your playfellow?
Mam.   No, I'll none of you.   5
1. La. Why, my sweet lord?
Mam. You'll kiss me hard and speak to me as if
I were a baby still. I love you better.
2. La. And why so, my lord?
Mam.   Not for because   10
Your brows are blacker; yet black brows, they say,
Become some women best, so that there be not
Too much hair there, but in a semicircle,
Or a half-moon made with a pen.
2. La.   Who taught 'this?   15
Mam. I learned it out of women's faces. Pray now
What color are your eyebrows?
1. La.   Blue, my lord.
Mam. Nay, that's a mock: I have seen a lady's nose
That has been blue, but not her eyebrows.   20

22

24. **wanton:** play.

27. **Good time encounter her:** may she have an easy delivery.

35. **sprites:** spirits.

43. **Yond crickets:** Hermione's tittering ladies.

1. La.   Hark ye!
The Queen your mother rounds apace. We shall
Present our services to a fine new prince
One of these days; and then you'ld wanton with us,
If we would have you.   25
    2. La.   She is spread of late
Into a goodly bulk. Good time encounter her!
  Her. What wisdom stirs amongst you? Come, sir,
    now
I am for you again. Pray you, sit by us,   30
And tell 's a tale.
  Mam.   Merry or sad shall 't be?
  Her. As merry as you will.
  Mam. A sad tale's best for winter: I have one
Of sprites and goblins.   35
  Her.   Let's have that, good sir.
Come on, sit down. Come on, and do your best
To fright me with your sprites; you're pow'rful at it.
  Mam. There was a man—
  Her.   Nay, come, sit down; then   40
    on.
  Mam. Dwelt by a churchyard. I will tell it softly:
Yond crickets shall not hear it.
  Her.   Come on, then,
And give 't me in mine ear.   45

[Enter Leontes, with Antigonus, Lords, and others.]

  Leon. Was he met there? his train? Camillo with
    him?
  1. Lo. Behind the tuft of pines I met them. Never

49. **scour:** scurry.

60. **hefts:** heaves.

61. **pander:** go-between.

63. **All's true that is mistrusted:** all my suspicions are proved true.

66. **pinched:** tortured: **very trick:** mere toy.

Saw I men scour so on their way. I eyed them
Even to their ships.   50
   Leon.   How blest am I
In my just censure, in my true opinion!
Alack, for lesser knowledge! How accursed
In being so blest! There may be in the cup
A spider steeped, and one may drink, depart,   55
And yet partake no venom; for his knowledge
Is not infected; but if one present
The abhorred ingredient to his eye, make known
How he hath drunk, he cracks his gorge, his sides,
With violent hefts. I have drunk, and seen the spider.   60
Camillo was his help in this, his pander.
There is a plot against my life, my crown;
All's true that is mistrusted. That false villain
Whom I employed was pre-employed by him.
He has discovered my design, and I   65
Remain a pinched thing; yea, a very trick
For them to play at will. How came the posterns
So easily open?
   1. Lo.   By his great authority,
Which often hath no less prevailed than so   70
On your command.
   Leon.   I know't too well.
Give me the boy. I am glad you did not nurse him.
Though he does bear some signs of me, yet you
Have too much blood in him.   75
   Her.   What is this? sport?
   Leon. Bear the boy hence; he shall not come about
     her.
Away with him! and let her sport herself

84. **lean to the nayward:** incline to the opposite opinion.

87. **goodly:** handsome.

89. **honest:** chaste.

90. **without-door form:** external appearance.

91. **straight:** immediately.

92. **brands:** marks of disgrace.

93. **I am out:** I say the wrong thing.

102. **replenished:** complete; perfect.

107. **a creature of thy place:** i.e., by a contemptuous term like "whore," or "strumpet."

With that she's big with; for 'tis Polixenes   80
Has made thee swell thus.

 Her.   But I'ld say he had not,
And I'll be sworn you would believe my saying,
Howe'er you lean to the nayward.

 Leon.   You, my lords,   85
Look on her, mark her well; be but about
To say, "She is a goodly lady," and
The justice of your hearts will thereto add,.
"'Tis pity she's not honest, honorable."
Praise her but for this her without-door form,   90
Which on my faith deserves high speech, and straight
The shrug, the hum or ha, these petty brands
That calumny doth use—oh, I am out—
That mercy does, for calumny will sear
Virtue itself: these shrugs, these hums and has,   95
When you have said, "She's goodly," come between
Ere you can say, "She's honest." But be't known,
From him that has most cause to grieve it should
  be,
She's an adult'ress.   100

 Her.   Should a villain say so,
The most replenished villain in the world,
He were as much more villain: you, my lord,
Do but mistake.

 Leon.   You have mistook, my lady,   105
Polixenes for Leontes. O thou thing!
Which I'll not call a creature of thy place,
Lest barbarism, making me the precedent,
Should a like language use to all degrees
And mannerly distinguishment leave out   110

114. **federary:** confederate; accomplice.
118. **vulgars:** common folk.
118-19. **privy/ To:** secretly informed of.
124. **throughly:** thoroughly.
128. **center:** center of the earth.
130-31. **is afar off guilty/ But that he speaks:** is at least remotely guilty merely in defending her.
140. **qualified:** tempered.

Betwixt the prince and beggar. I have said
She's an adult'ress; I have said with whom.
More, she's a traitor, and Camillo is
A federary with her and one that knows
What she should shame to know herself   115
But with her most vile principal: that she's
A bed swerver, even as bad as those
That vulgars give bold'st titles; ay, and privy
To this their late escape.

Her.   No, by my life,   120
Privy to none of this. How will this grieve you,
When you shall come to clearer knowledge, that
You thus have published me! Gentle my lord,
You scarce can right me throughly, then, to say
You did mistake.   125

Leon.   No; if I mistake
In those foundations which I build upon,
The center is not big enough to bear
A schoolboy's top. Away with her to prison!
He who shall speak for her is afar off guilty   130
But that he speaks.

Her.   There's some ill planet reigns:
I must be patient till the heavens look
With an aspect more favorable. Good my lords,
I am not prone to weeping, as our sex   135
Commonly are; the want of which vain dew
Perchance shall dry your pities; but I have
That honorable grief lodged here which burns
Worse than tears drown. Beseech you all, my lords,
With thoughts so qualified as your charities   140

143. **Shall I be heard:** will no one hear my command. There has been no move to bear Hermione to prison as he ordered in line 129.

147. **fools:** a term of affection rather than contempt.

148-50. **When you shall know your mistress/ Has deserved prison, then abound in tears/ As I come out:** i.e., it would be occasion for distress if you knew me guilty and saw me freed.

150-51. **This action I now go on/ Is for my better grace:** Hermione thinks of the proverbial idea that unmerited afflictions are sent by God for one's good.

153. **leave:** permission.

166. **in couples:** i.e., yoked together, like animals.

Shall best instruct you, measure me; and so
The King's will be performed!

    Leon. [*To the Guard*]   Shall I be heard?

    Her. Who is't that goes with me? Beseech your
    Highness,   145
My women may be with me; for you see
My plight requires it. Do not weep, good fools;
There is no cause. When you shall know your mistress
Has deserved prison, then abound in tears
As I come out. This action I now go on   150
Is for my better grace. Adieu, my lord.
I never wished to see you sorry; now
I trust I shall. My women, come; you have leave.

    Leon. Go, do our bidding; hence!

          [*Exit Queen, guarded, with Ladies.*]

    1. Lo. Beseech your Highness, call the Queen again. 155

    Ant. Be certain what you do, sir, lest your justice
Prove violence; in the which three great ones suffer,
Yourself, your queen, your son.

    1. Lo.   For her, my lord,
I dare my life lay down and will do't, sir,   160
Please you t' accept it, that the Queen is spotless
I' the eyes of Heaven and to you—I mean,
In this which you accuse her.

    Ant.   If it prove
She's otherwise, I'll keep my stables where   165
I lodge my wife; I'll go in couples with her;
Than when I feel and see her no farther trust her;
For every inch of woman in the world—
Ay, every dram of woman's flesh—is false,
If she be.   170

174. **abused:** deceived: **putter-on:** inciter.

176. **land-damn him:** Antigonus has just said that the villain will be damned; in the meantime he will make him taste hell on earth.

180. **geld:** spay; deprive of ovaries, possibly with secondary sense "cut off," as is done to superfluous shoots of a plant.

181. **false generations:** illegitimate children.

182. **glib:** geld. Antigonus means that he would deprive himself of a posterity to inherit his land, which would be the effect of preventing his daughters from having children.

183. **fair issue:** honest (legitimate) offspring.

193. **lack I credit:** am I disbelieved.

200. **Our forceful instigation:** my strong impulse.

Leon. Hold your peaces.

1. Lo.   Good my lord—

Ant. It is for you we speak, not for ourselves.
You are abused and by some putter-on
That will be damned for't. Would I knew the villain, 175
I would land-damn him. Be she honor-flawed—
I have three daughters; the eldest is eleven;
The second and the third, nine, and some five—
If this prove true, they'll pay for't. By mine honor,
I'll geld 'em all; fourteen they shall not see   180
To bring false generations. They are co-heirs;
And I had rather glib myself than they
Should not produce fair issue.

Leon.   Cease! no more.
You smell this business with a sense as cold   185
As is a dead man's nose; but I do see't and feel't
As you feel doing thus; and see withal
The instruments that feel.

Ant.   If it be so,
We need no grave to bury honesty.   190
There's not a grain of it the face to sweeten
Of the whole dungy earth.

Leon.   What! lack I credit?

1. Lo. I had rather you did lack than I, my lord,
Upon this ground; and more it would content me 195
To have her honor true than your suspicion,
Be blamed for't how you might.

Leon.   Why, what need we
Commune with you of this, but rather follow
Our forceful instigation? Our prerogative   200
Calls not your counsels, but our natural goodness

203. **skill:** cunning.

207. **Properly:** personally mine.

210. **overture:** disclosure.

215. **gross:** evident.

216. **approbation:** proof.

218. **Made up to the deed:** adding up to the certainty of the deed.

221. **wild:** rash; **in post:** with all haste, literally, by post horses.

222. **Delphos:** one of the Greek islands called Delos, the reputed birthplace of Apollo, was known to Shakespeare and his contemporaries as Delphos. The oracle referred to was at Apollo's shrine on the island rather than at the more famous Delphi.

224. **stuffed sufficiency:** ample competence.

225. **had:** received.

The tripod of Apollo's oracle. From Vincenzo Cartari, *Imagini de gli dei delli antichi* (1615).

Imparts this; which, if you, or stupefied
Or seeming so in skill, cannot or will not
Relish a truth like us, inform yourselves
We need no more of your advice. The matter,   205
The loss, the gain, the ord'ring on't, is all
Properly ours.

    Ant.   And I wish, my Liege,
You had only in your silent judgment tried it,
Without more overture.   210

    Leon.   How could that be?
Either thou art most ignorant by age,
Or thou wert born a fool. Camillo's flight,
Added to their familiarity—
Which was as gross as ever touched conjecture,   215
That lacked sight only, nought for approbation
But only seeing, all other circumstances
Made up to the deed—doth push on this proceeding.
Yet, for a greater confirmation—
For in an act of this importance 'twere   220
Most piteous to be wild—I have dispatched in post
To sacred Delphos, to Apollo's temple,
Cleomenes and Dion, whom you know
Of stuffed sufficiency. Now from the oracle
They will bring all; whose spiritual counsel had   225
Shall stop or spur me. Have I done well?

    1. Lo. Well done, my lord.

    Leon. Though I am satisfied and need no more
Than what I know, yet shall the oracle
Give rest to the minds of others, such as he   230
Whose ignorant credulity will not
Come up to the truth. So have we thought it good

233. **free:** freely accessible.
237. **raise:** stir.

||||||||||||||||||||||||||||||||||||||||||||||||||||||||||

II.ii. Paulina, Antigonus' wife and attendant to Hermione, visits the prison and demands to see the Queen. She discovers that Hermione has prematurely given birth to a daughter and orders the jailer to bring her the child in the hope that the sight of her will convince Leontes of his mistake.

From our free person she should be confined,
Lest that the treachery of the two fled hence
Be left her to perform. Come, follow us.   235
We are to speak in public; for this business
Will raise us all.

    Ant. [*Aside*] To laughter, as I take it,
If the good truth were known.

                           Exeunt.

Scene II. [A prison.]

Enter Paulina, a Gentleman, [and Attendants].

    Paul. The keeper of the prison, call to him;
Let him have knowledge who I am.

                      [*Exit Gentleman.*]
                        Good lady,
No court in Europe is too good for thee;
What dost thou then in prison?   5

[Enter Gentleman, with the Jailer.]

                      Now, good sir,
You know me, do you not?

    Jail.   For a worthy lady
And one who much I honor.

    Paul.   Pray you, then,   10
Conduct me to the Queen.

    Jail.   I may not, madam:
To the contrary I have express commandment.

18. **So please you:** if it please you to.

27. **As passes coloring:** such as surpasses any skill to conceal it.

31. **On:** as a result of.

Paul. Here's ado,
To lock up honesty and honor from   15
The access of gentle visitors! Is't lawful, pray you,
To see her women? Any of them? Emilia?
   Jail. So please you, madam,
To put apart these your attendants, I
Shall bring Emilia forth.   20
   Paul.   I pray now, call her.
Withdraw yourselves.
                    [*Exeunt Gentleman and Attendants.*]
   Jail.   And, madam,
I must be present at your conference.
   Paul. Well, be't so, prithee.   [*Exit Jailer.*] 25
Here's such ado to make no stain a stain
As passes coloring.

                [*Enter Jailer, with Emilia.*]

                    Dear gentlewoman,
How fares our gracious lady?
   Em. As well as one so great and so forlorn   30
May hold together. On her frights and griefs,
Which never tender lady hath borne greater,
She is something before her time delivered.
   Paul. A boy?
   Em. A daughter, and a goodly babe,   35
Lusty and like to live. The Queen receives
Much comfort in't; says, "My poor prisoner,
I am innocent as you."
   Paul.   I dare be sworn.

40. **lunes:** fits of madness.

44. **blister:** referring to the proverb "Fair words blister not the tongue."

47. **Commend:** offer.

56. **free:** generous; **miss:** lack; fail to achieve.

57. **issue:** result.

58. **meet:** suitable.

59. **presently:** at once.

61. **hammered of:** wrought over in her mind.

65. **wit:** persuasive speech.

These dangerous unsafe lunes i' the King, beshrew   40
      them!
He must be told on't, and he shall. The office
Becomes a woman best; I'll take't upon me.
If I prove honey-mouthed, let my tongue blister,
And never to my red-looked anger be   45
The trumpet any more. Pray you, Emilia,
Commend my best obedience to the Queen.
If she dares trust me with her little babe,
I'll show't the King and undertake to be
Her advocate to the loud'st. We do not know   50
How he may soften at the sight o' the child:
The silence often of pure innocence
Persuades when speaking fails.
      Em.   Most worthy madam.
Your honor and your goodness is so evident   55
That your free undertaking cannot miss
A thriving issue. There is no lady living
So meet for this great errand. Please your Ladyship
To visit the next room, I'll presently
Acquaint the Queen of your most noble offer;   60
Who but today hammered of this design,
But durst not tempt a minister of honor,
Lest she should be denied.
      Paul.   Tell her, Emilia,
I'll use that tongue I have. If wit flow from't   65
As boldness from my bosom, let't not be doubted
I shall do good.
      Em.   Now be you blest for it!
I'll to the Queen. Please you, come something nearer.
      Jail. Madam, if't please the Queen to send the babe, 70

75. law and process: legal process.

||||||||||||||||||||||||||||||||||||||||||||||||||||||||

II.iii. Since Leontes cannot touch Polixenes, he is determined to make Hermione suffer for her infidelity. Mamillius has fallen ill and Leontes attributes the boy's ailment to shame at his mother's dishonor. When Paulina enters with the infant daughter, Leontes refuses to accept it as his child, although she points out its close resemblance to himself. He blames Antigonus for Paulina's interference and orders him to take the child and expose it in some deserted place outside his own realm. Antigonus reluctantly takes the babe away. Leontes is informed that Cleomenes and Dion have returned with the oracle's verdict and orders a public arraignment of Hermione.

||||||||||||||||||||||||||||||||||||||||||||||

1. Nor: neither.
4. harlot: lewd.
5. blank: literally, center of the target.
6. level: aim.
8. Given to the fire: burning alive was the punishment at one time for husband murder, actual or attempted, which was regarded as a form of treason; **moiety:** portion.

I know not what I shall incur to pass it,
Having no warrant.
   Paul.   You need not fear it, sir.
This child was prisoner to the womb and is
By law and process of great Nature thence   75
Freed and enfranchised; not a party to
The anger of the King, nor guilty of,
If any be, the trespass of the Queen.
   Jail. I do believe it.
   Paul. Do not you fear. Upon mine honor, I   80
Will stand betwixt you and danger.

                                  Exeunt.

Scene III. [A room in Leontes' palace.]

Enter Leontes, Antigonus, Lords, and Servants.

   Leon. Nor night nor day no rest: it is but weakness
To bear the matter thus; mere weakness. If
The cause were not in being—part o' the cause,
She, the adult'ress; for the harlot King
Is quite beyond mine arm, out of the blank   5
And level of my brain, plot-proof; but she
I can hook to me: say that she were gone,
Given to the fire, a moiety of my rest
Might come to me again. Who's there?
   1. Ser.   My lord?   10
   Leon. How does the boy?
   1. Ser.   He took good rest tonight:
'Tis hoped his sickness is discharged.

21. **him:** i.e., Polixenes.
24. **parties:** allies; **alliance:** kinship.
31. **be second to me:** assist me.
32. **tyrannous:** fierce.
34. **free:** innocent.

Leon. To see his nobleness!
Conceiving the dishonor of his mother,   15
He straight declined, drooped, took it deeply,
Fastened and fixed the shame on't in himself,
Threw off his spirit, his appetite, his sleep,
And downright languished. Leave me solely: go,
See how he fares. [*Exit Servant.*] Fie, fie! no thought   20
   of him!
The very thought of my revenges that way
Recoil upon me: in himself too mighty,
And in his parties, his alliance. Let him be
Until a time may serve: for present vengeance,   25
Take it on her. Camillo and Polixenes
Laugh at me, make their pastime at my sorrow.
They should not laugh if I could reach them, nor
Shall she within my pow'r.

Enter Paulina, [with a child].

1. Lo.   You must not enter.   30
   Paul. Nay, rather, good my lords, be second to me.
Fear you his tyrannous passion more, alas,
Than the Queen's life? a gracious, innocent soul,
More free than he is jealous.
   Ant.   That's enough.   35
   2. Ser. Madam, he hath not slept tonight, com-
      manded
None should come at him.
   Paul.   Not so hot, good sir:
I come to bring him sleep. 'Tis such as you,   40
That creep like shadows by him and do sigh

42. **heavings:** spasms.

43. **the cause of his awaking:** i.e., the wild fancies that keep him wakeful.

49. **gossips:** godparents.

60. **Commit me for committing honor:** imprison me for acting honorably.

64. **she'll not stumble:** she can be relied upon to behave honorably.

68-9. **dares/ Less appear so in comforting your evils:** dares appear less so by not aiding you in doing wrong.

At each his needless heavings, such as you
Nourish the cause of his awaking. I
Do come with words as medicinal as true,
Honest as either, to purge him of that humor   45
That presses him from sleep.

    Leon.   What noise there, ho?

    Paul. No noise, my lord; but needful conference
About some gossips for your Highness.

    Leon.   Howl   50
Away with that audacious lady! Antigonus,
I charged thee that she should not come about me:
I knew she would.

    Ant.   I told her so, my lord,
On your displeasure's peril and on mine,   55
She should not visit you.

    Leon.   What, canst not rule her?

    Paul. From all dishonesty he can. In this,
Unless he take the course that you have done,
Commit me for committing honor, trust it,   60
He shall not rule me.

    Ant.   La you now, you hear.
When she will take the rein I let her run;
But she'll not stumble.

    Paul.   Good my Liege, I come;   65
And, I beseech you, hear me, who professes
Myself your loyal servant, your physician,
Your most obedient counselor, yet that dares
Less appear so in comforting your evils
Than such as most seem yours. I say, I come   70
From your good queen.

    Leon.   Good queen!

75. **by combat make her good:** prove her innocence by combat, as was common among knights of chivalry.

76. **worst about you:** least valiant of your companions.

78. **makes but trifles of his eyes:** values his eyes so little that he will expose them to Paulina's nails.

84. **mankind:** scolding; virago-like.

85. **intelligencing bawd:** messenger for illicit lovers.

94. **Dame Partlet:** name for the hen in Chaucer's "Nun's Priest's Tale."

98. **by that forced baseness:** i.e., at Leontes' order to take up **the bastard,** a name unjustly applied to the child.

Paul.   Good queen, my lord,
Good queen; I say good queen:
And would by combat make her good, so were I   75
A man, the worst about you.
    Leon.   Force her hence.
    Paul. Let him that makes but trifles of his eyes
First hand me. On mine own accord I'll off,
But first I'll do my errand. The good queen,   80
For she is good, hath brought you forth a daughter;
Here 'tis; commends it to your blessing.
                    [*Laying down the child.*]
    Leon.   Out!
A mankind witch! Hence with her, out o' door!
A most intelligencing bawd!   85
    Paul.   Not so:
I am as ignorant in that as you
In so entitling me, and no less honest
Than you are mad; which is enough, I'll warrant,
As this world goes, to pass for honest.   90
    Leon.   Traitors!
Will you not push her out? Give her the bastard.
Thou dotard! thou art woman-tired, unroosted
By thy Dame Partlet here. Take up the bastard!
Take't up, I say! Give't to thy crone.   95
    Paul.   Forever
Unvenerable be thy hands, if thou
Takest up the Princess by that forced baseness
Which he has put upon't!
    Leon.   He dreads his wife.   100
    Paul. So I would you did: then 'twere past all
    doubt

111. **as the case now stands, it is a curse:** we are plagued by the fact of his royal authority.

115. **callet:** scold; often, specifically, the loose female companion of beggars.

116-17. **beat . . . baits:** pronounced similarly.

122. **proverb:** "They are so like that they are the worse for it."

124. **print:** copy.

130. **got:** begot.

132. **yellow:** i.e., tinge of jealousy. Paulina means that if the child inherited any of Leontes' jealousy, she might be mad enough to doubt her own fidelity to her husband.

You'd call your children yours.

    Leon.   A nest of traitors!

    Ant. I am none, by this good light.   105

    Paul.   Nor I, nor any

But one that's here, and that's himself; for he

The sacred honor of himself, his queen's,

His hopeful son's, his babe's, betrays to slander,

Whose sting is sharper than the sword's; and will not— 110

For, as the case now stands, it is a curse

He cannot be compelled to't—once remove

The root of his opinion, which is rotten

As ever oak or stone was sound.

    Leon.   A callet   115

Of boundless tongue, who late hath beat her husband

And now baits me! This brat is none of mine:

It is the issue of Polixenes.

Hence with it, and together with the dam

Commit them to the fire!   120

    Paul.   It is yours;

And, might we lay the old proverb to your charge,

So like you, 'tis the worse. Behold, my lords,

Although the print be little, the whole matter

And copy of the father, eye, nose, lip;   125

The trick of's frown; his forehead; nay, the valley,

The pretty dimples of his chin and cheek; his smiles;

The very mold and frame of hand, nail, finger.

And thou, good goddess Nature, which hast made it

So like to him that got it, if thou hast   130

The ordering of the mind too, 'mongst all colors

No yellow in't, lest she suspect, as he does,

Her children not her husband's!

135. **lozel:** good-for-nothing.

159. **better:** i.e., better than that of Leontes;
What needs these hands: you need not lay hands
on me.

Leon.   A gross hag!
And, lozel, thou art worthy to be hanged   135
That wilt not stay her tongue.

Ant.   Hang all the husbands
That cannot do that feat, you'll leave yourself
Hardly one subject.

Leon.   Once more, take her hence.   140

Paul. A most unworthy and unnatural lord
Can do no more.

Leon.   I'll ha' thee burnt.

Paul.   I care not:
It is an heretic that makes the fire,   145
Not she which burns in't. I'll not call you tyrant;
But this most cruel usage of your queen—
Not able to produce more accusation
Than your own weak-hinged fancy—something sa-
    vors   150
Of tyranny and will ignoble make you,
Yea, scandalous to the world.

Leon.   On your allegiance,
Out of the chamber with her! Were I a tyrant,
Where were her life? She durst not call me so,   155
If she did know me one. Away with her!

Paul. I pray you, do not push me: I'll be gone.
Look to your babe, my lord; 'tis yours. Jove send her
A better guiding spirit! What needs these hands?
You, that are thus so tender o'er his follies,   160
Will never do him good, not one of you.
So, so. Farewell; we are gone.   *Exit.*

Leon. Thou, traitor, hast set on thy wife to this.
My child? Away with't! Even thou, that hast

172. **proper:** personal.

174. **settst on:** incited.

182. **beseech':** the apostrophe indicates omission of the pronoun "you."

194. **Lady Margery:** a common name among women who served as midwives.

A heart so tender o'er it, take it hence   165
And see it instantly consumed with fire;
Even thou and none but thou. Take it up straight!
Within this hour bring me word 'tis done,
And by good testimony, or I'll seize thy life,
With what thou else callst thine. If thou refuse   170
And wilt encounter with my wrath, say so:
The bastard brains with these my proper hands
Shall I dash out. Go, take it to the fire;
For thou settst on thy wife.

  Ant.   I did not, sir.   175
These lords, my noble fellows, if they please,
Can clear me in't.

  Lords.   We can. My royal Liege,
He is not guilty of her coming hither.

  Leon. You're liars all.   180

  1. Lo. Beseech your Highness, give us better credit.
We have always truly served you; and beseech'
So to esteem of us; and on our knees we beg,
As recompense of our dear services
Past and to come, that you do change this purpose,   185
Which, being so horrible, so bloody, must
Lead on to some foul issue. We all kneel.

  Leon. I am a feather for each wind that blows.
Shall I live on to see this bastard kneel
And call me father? Better burn it now   190
Than curse it then. But be it: let it live—
It shall not neither. You, sir, come you hither;
You that have been so tenderly officious
With Lady Margery, your midwife there,
To save this bastard's life—for 'tis a bastard,   195

206. **seest thou:** do you understand.

214. **it:** common form of the neuter genitive; its.

218. **strangely to some place:** to some place outside Sicilia.

225-26. **be prosperous/ In more than this deed does require:** may you have better luck than you merit by this deed.

So sure as this beard's gray—what will you adventure
To save this brat's life?
    Ant.   Anything, my lord,
That my ability may undergo,
And nobleness impose: at least thus much—   200
I'll pawn the little blood which I have left
To save the innocent. Anything possible.
    Leon. It shall be possible. Swear by this sword
Thou wilt perform my bidding.
    Ant.   I will, my lord.   205
    Leon. Mark and perform it: seest thou? For the fail
Of any point in't shall not only be
Death to thyself but to thy lewd-tongued wife,
Whom for this time we pardon. We enjoin thee,
As thou art liegeman to us, that thou carry   210
This female bastard hence, and that thou bear it
To some remote and desert place, quite out
Of our dominions; and that there thou leave it,
Without more mercy, to it own protection
And favor of the climate. As by strange fortune   215
It came to us, I do in justice charge thee,
On thy soul's peril and thy body's torture,
That thou commend it strangely to some place
Where chance may nurse or end it. Take it up.
    Ant. I swear to do this, though a present death   220
Had been more merciful. Come on, poor babe:
Some powerful spirit instruct the kites and ravens
To be thy nurses! Wolves and bears, they say,
Casting their savageness aside, have done
Like offices of pity. Sir, be prosperous   225
In more than this deed does require! And blessing

228. **loss:** destruction.
231. **posts:** messengers.
237. **accompt:** accounting for.

Against this cruelty fight on thy side,
Poor thing, condemned to loss!   *Exit [with the child].*
 Leon.   No, I'll not rear
Another's issue.   230

     Enter a Servant.

 Ser.   Please your Highness, posts
From those you sent to the oracle are come
An hour since. Cleomenes and Dion,
Being well arrived from Delphos, are both landed,
Hasting to the court.   235
 1. Lo.   So please you, sir, their speed
Hath been beyond accompt.
 Leon.   Twenty-three days
They have been absent. 'Tis good speed; foretells
The great Apollo suddenly will have   240
The truth of this appear. Prepare you, lords;
Summon a session, that we may arraign
Our most disloyal lady; for, as she hath
Been publicly accused, so shall she have
A just and open trial. While she lives 245
My heart will be a burden to me. Leave me,
And think upon my bidding.
          Exeunt.

THE
WINTER'S
TALE

ACT III

III.i. Cleomenes and Dion engage horses at a Sicilian seaport to hasten to Leontes with the words of the oracle. They hope Hermione will soon be cleared of the charges publicly proclaimed throughout the kingdom.

━━━━━━━━━━━━━━━

5. **habits:** garments.
10. **of all:** most of all.
12. **surprised:** overcame.
14. **event:** outcome.

ACT III

Scene I. [A seaport in Sicilia.]

Enter Cleomenes and Dion.

Cleo. The climate's delicate, the air most sweet,
Fertile the isle, the temple much surpassing
The common praise it bears.
Dion.   I shall report,
For most it caught me, the celestial habits,   5
Methinks I so should term them, and the reverence
Of the grave wearers. Oh, the sacrifice!
How ceremonious, solemn, and unearthly
It was i' the off'ring!
Cleo.   But of all, the burst   10
And the ear-deaf'ning voice o' the oracle,
Kin to Jove's thunder, so surprised my sense
That I was nothing.
Dion.   If the event o' the journey
Prove as successful to the Queen—oh, be't so!—   15
As it hath been to us rare, pleasant, speedy,
The time is worth the use on't.
Cleo.   Great Apollo
Turn all to the best! These proclamations,

42

22. **violent carriage:** hasty management.
24. **divine:** priest.
25. **discover:** reveal.
27. **gracious:** favorable; fortunate.

<hr/>

III.ii. At the public hearing of Hermione's case, she denies Leontes' accusation of adultery and conspiracy against his life. She has no expectation that Leontes will believe her denial but hopes that the oracle will clear her honor. Since she has been separated from her son and her newborn daughter is to be killed, she has no wish to save her life. Cleomenes and Dion present the oracle's statement, which declares that Hermione, Polixenes, and Camillo are innocent of Leontes' charges; the infant is Leontes'; and that he will live without an heir if "that which is lost be not found." Leontes refuses to believe the oracle, but when a servant reports that Mamillius has died and Hermione faints, he suddenly comes to his senses. Paulina and other ladies escort Hermione from the room, and Paulina returns to announce that Hermione is also dead. The penitent Leontes vows to do daily penance at the grave of his wife and son.

So forcing faults upon Hermione,   20
I little like.

  Dion.   The violent carriage of it
Will clear or end the business. When the oracle,
Thus by Apollo's great divine sealed up,
Shall the contents discover, something rare   25
Even then will rush to knowledge. Go: fresh horses!
And gracious be the issue!

                                        Exeunt.

Scene II. [A court of justice.]

Enter Leontes, Lords, and Officers.

  Leon. This sessions, to our great grief we pro-
      nounce,
Even pushes 'gainst our heart: the party tried
The daughter of a king, our wife, and one
Of us too much beloved. Let us be cleared   5
Of being tyrannous, since we so openly
Proceed in justice, which shall have due course,
Even to the guilt or the purgation.
Produce the prisoner.

  Off. It is His Highness' pleasure that the Queen   10
Appear in person here in court. Silence!

[*Enter Hermione guarded; Paulina and Ladies
          attending.*]

  Leon. Read the indictment.
  Off. [*Reads*] "Hermione, queen to the worthy Leon-

18. **pretense:** intention.
26. **boot:** avail; profit.
37. **history:** story; romance.
38. **take:** charm.
39. **owe:** possess.
44. **weigh:** prize.

tes, King of Sicilia, thou art here accused and ar-
raigned of high treason, in committing adultery with   15
Polixenes, King of Bohemia, and conspiring with
Camillo to take away the life of our sovereign lord,
the King, thy royal husband: the pretense whereof
being by circumstances partly laid open, thou, Hermione, contrary to the faith and allegiance of a true   20
subject, didst counsel and aid them, for their better
safety, to fly away by night."

 Her. Since what I am to say must be but that
Which contradicts my accusation, and
The testimony on my part no other   25
But what comes from myself, it shall scarce boot me
To say, "Not guilty." Mine integrity,
Being counted falsehood, shall, as I express it,
Be so received. But thus: if pow'rs divine
Behold our human actions, as they do,   30
I doubt not then but innocence shall make
False accusation blush and tyranny
Tremble at patience. You, my lord, best know,
Who least will seem to do so, my past life
Hath been as continent, as chaste, as true,   35
As I am now unhappy; which is more
Than history can pattern, though devised
And played to take spectators. For behold me,
A fellow of the royal bed, which owe
A moiety of the throne, a great king's daughter,   40
The mother to a hopeful prince, here standing
To prate and talk for life and honor 'fore
Who please to come and hear. For life, I prize it
As I weigh grief, which I would spare. For honor,

45-6. a derivative from me to mine,/ And only that I stand for: something handed down to my children, and that is what I am concerned to defend.

50-1. With what encounter so uncurrent I/ Have strained, t' appear thus: how I have strained the limits of lawful social behavior that I should be thus forced to defend my honor.

61. due: owing; relevant.

62. own: admit.

63-4. More than mistress of/ Which comes to me in name of fault: more than what I have really done, which is now charged against me as a fault.

67. as in honor he required: i.e., with the respect proper to his position.

'Tis a derivative from me to mine,   45
And only that I stand for. I appeal
To your own conscience, sir, before Polixenes
Came to your court, how I was in your grace,
How merited to be so; since he came,
With what encounter so uncurrent I   50
Have strained, t' appear thus: if one jot beyond
The bound of honor, or in act or will
That way inclining, hardened be the hearts
Of all that hear me, and my near'st of kin
Cry fie upon my grave!   55
    Leon.   I ne'er heard yet
That any of these bolder vices wanted
Less impudence to gainsay what they did
Than to perform it first.
    Her.   That's true enough;   60
Though 'tis a saying, sir, not due to me.
    Leon. You will not own it.
    Her.   More than mistress of
Which comes to me in name of fault, I must not
At all acknowledge. For Polixenes,   65
With whom I am accused, I do confess
I loved him as in honor he required,
With such a kind of love as might become
A lady like me, with a love even such,
So and no other, as yourself commanded: 70
Which not to have done, I think, had been in me
Both disobedience and ingratitude
To you and toward your friend, whose love had spoke,
Even since it could speak, from an infant, freely
That it was yours. Now, for conspiracy,   75

80. **Wotting no more than I:** unless they know more than I.

85. **in the level of your dreams:** at the mercy of your fancies.

90. **of your fact:** guilty of your crime.

91. **concerns more than avails:** you make more important than the good it will do you; denials will carry no weight with Leontes.

92. **itself:** i.e., an outcast.

98. **bug:** bogey.

99. **commodity:** advantage; pleasure.

100. **crown and comfort:** crowning happiness.

101. **give lost:** give up for lost.

105. **Starred most unluckily:** born under a most unlucky star.

I know not how it tastes, though it be dished
For me to try how. All I know of it
Is that Camillo was an honest man;
And why he left your court, the gods themselves,
Wotting no more than I, are ignorant.   80

   Leon. You knew of his departure, as you know
What you have underta'en to do in's absence.

   Her. Sir,
You speak a language that I understand not.
My life stands in the level of your dreams,   85
Which I'll lay down.

   Leon.   Your actions are my dreams.
You had a bastard by Polixenes,
And I but dreamed it. As you were past all shame—
Those of your fact are so—so past all truth;   90
Which to deny concerns more than avails; for as
Thy brat hath been cast out, like to itself,
No father owning it—which is, indeed,
More criminal in thee than it—so thou
Shalt feel our justice, in whose easiest passage   95
Look for no less than death.

   Her.   Sir, spare your threats.
The bug which you would fright me with I seek:
To me can life be no commodity.
The crown and comfort of my life, your favor,   100
I do give lost; for I do feel it gone,
But know not how it went. My second joy
And first fruits of my body, from his presence
I am barred, like one infectious. My third comfort,
Starred most unluckily, is from my breast,   105
The innocent milk in it most innocent mouth,

109. **'longs:** belongs.

110. **all fashion:** every class.

112. **strength of limit:** the strength regained by resting a set term after delivery of a child.

117. **free:** clear.

119. **jealousies:** suspicions.

121. **refer me:** submit myself.

129. **flatness:** completeness.

Haled out to murder: myself on every post
Proclaimed a strumpet; with immodest hatred
The childbed privilege denied, which 'longs
To women of all fashion; lastly, hurried   110
Here to this place, i' the open air, before
I have got strength of limit. Now, my Liege,
Tell me what blessings I have here alive
That I should fear to die? Therefore proceed.
But yet hear this—mistake me not: no life,   115
I prize it not a straw, but for mine honor,
Which I would free, if I shall be condemned
Upon surmises, all proofs sleeping else
But what your jealousies awake, I tell you
'Tis rigor and not law. Your Honors all,   120
I do refer me to the oracle.
Apollo be my judge!
  1. Lo.   This your request
Is altogether just: therefore bring forth,
And in Apollo's name, his oracle. [*Exeunt Officers.*] 125
  Her. The Emperor of Russia was my father.
Oh that he were alive and here beholding
His daughter's trial! that he did but see
The flatness of my misery, yet with eyes
Of pity, not revenge!   130

    [*Enter Officers, with Cleomenes and Dion.*]

  Off. You here shall swear upon this sword of justice
That you, Cleomenes and Dion, have
Been both at Delphos and from thence have brought

155. **conceit and fear:** fearful imagination.
156. **speed:** fare.

This sealed-up oracle, by the hand delivered
Of great Apollo's priest, and that since then   135
You have not dared to break the holy seal
Nor read the secrets in't.

    Cleo., Dion.   All this we swear.

    Leon. Break up the seals and read.

    Off. [*Reads*] "Hermione is chaste; Polixenes blame- 140
less; Camillo a true subject; Leontes a jealous tyrant;
his innocent babe truly begotten; and the King shall
live without an heir, if that which is lost be not
found."

    Lords. Now blessed be the great Apollo!   145

    Her.   Praised!

    Leon. Hast thou read truth?

    Off.   Ay, my lord, even so
As it is here set down.

    Leon. There is no truth at all i' the oracle!   150
The sessions shall proceed: this is mere falsehood.

[*Enter Servant.*]

    Ser. My lord the King, the King!

    Leon.   What is the business?

    Ser. O sir, I shall be hated to report it!
The Prince, your son, with mere conceit and fear   155
Of the Queen's speed, is gone.

    Leon.   How! gone!

    Ser.   Is dead.

    Leon. Apollo's angry; and the Heavens themselves
Do strike at my injustice. [*Hermione faints.*] How   160
    now there!

165. **o'ercharged:** overburdened.
178. **tardied:** delayed.
183. **Unclasped my practice:** revealed my plot.
185. **commended:** submitted.
186. **No richer than his honor:** owning nothing but his honor; i.e., leaving all his worldly possessions behind; **glisters:** shines.
187. **Through my rust:** through the tarnish I cast on his honor.

Paul. This news is mortal to the Queen. Look down
And see what death is doing.

Leon.   Take her hence.
Her heart is but o'ercharged; she will recover.   165
I have too much believed mine own suspicion.
Beseech you, tenderly apply to her
Some remedies for life.

          [*Exeunt Paulina and Ladies, with Hermione.*]
                    Apollo, pardon
My great profaneness 'gainst thine oracle!   170
I'll reconcile me to Polixenes;
New woo my queen; recall the good Camillo,
Whom I proclaim a man of truth, of mercy;
For, being transported by my jealousies
To bloody thoughts and to revenge, I chose   175
Camillo for the minister to poison
My friend Polixenes: which had been done
But that the good mind of Camillo tardied
My swift command, though I with death and with
Reward did threaten and encourage him,   180
Not doing it and being done. He, most humane
And filled with honor, to my kingly guest
Unclasped my practice, quit his fortunes here,
Which you knew great, and to the hazard
Of all incertainties himself commended,   185
No richer than his honor. How he glisters
Through my rust! and how his piety
Does my deeds make the blacker!

               [*Enter Paulina.*]

193. **studied:** carefully planned.

202. **spices:** slight traces.

204. **show thee, of a fool:** demonstrate thee an example of a fool.

207-8. **poor trespasses,/ More monstrous standing by:** minor offenses, compared with the monstrous ones to come.

215. **gross and foolish:** greatly foolish.

218. **said:** finished speaking.

Paul.   Woe the while!
Oh, cut my lace, lest my heart, cracking it,   190
Break too!
    1. Lo. What fit is this, good lady?
    Paul. What studied torments, tyrant, hast for me?
What wheels? racks? fires? what flaying? boiling?
In leads or oils? What old or newer torture   195
Must I receive, whose every word deserves
To taste of thy most worst? Thy tyranny
Together working with thy jealousies,
Fancies too weak for boys, too green and idle
For girls of nine, oh, think what they have done   200
And then run mad indeed, stark mad! for all
Thy bygone fooleries were but spices of it.
That thou betrayedst Polixenes, 'twas nothing;
That did but show thee, of a fool, inconstant
And damnable ingrateful. Nor was't much,   205
Thou wouldst have poisoned good Camillo's honor,
To have him kill a king; poor trespasses,
More monstrous standing by: whereof I reckon
The casting forth to crows thy baby daughter
To be or none or little, though a devil   210
Would have shed water out of fire ere done't:
Nor is't directly laid to thee the death
Of the young Prince, whose honorable thoughts,
Thoughts high for one so tender, cleft the heart
That could conceive a gross and foolish sire   215
Blemished his gracious dam. This is not, no,
Laid to thy answer; but the last—O lords,
When I have said, cry "woe!"—the Queen, the Queen,

230. **knees:** kneeling in prayer.

231. **together:** consecutively.

232. **still:** ever.

245-46. **What's gone and what's past help/ Should be past grief:** cf. the proverb "Past cure, past care."

246-47. **Do not receive affliction/ At my petition:** do not let my appeal distress you.

248. **minded:** reminded.

The sweet'st, dear'st creature's dead, and vengeance
    for't   220
Not dropped down yet.
    1. Lo.   The higher pow'rs forbid!
    Paul. I say she's dead, I'll swear't. If word nor oath
Prevail not, go and see. If you can bring
Tincture or luster in her lip, her eye,   225
Heat outwardly or breath within, I'll serve you
As I would do the gods. But, O thou tyrant!
Do not repent these things, for they are heavier
Than all thy woes can stir. Therefore betake thee
To nothing but despair. A thousand knees   230
Ten thousand years together, naked, fasting,
Upon a barren mountain, and still winter
In storm perpetual, could not move the gods
To look that way thou wert.
    Leon.   Go on, go on!   235
Thou canst not speak too much: I have deserved
All tongues to talk their bitt'rest.
    1. Lo.   Say no more:
Howe'er the business goes, you have made fault
I' the boldness of your speech.   240
    Paul.   I am sorry for't:
All faults I make, when I shall come to know them,
I do repent. Alas! I have showed too much
The rashness of a woman. He is touched
To the noble heart. What's gone and what's past help 245
Should be past grief. Do not receive affliction
At my petition: I beseech you, rather
Let me be punished that have minded you

262. **Our:** my.

264. **recreation:** refreshment of spirit; comfort.

267. **sorrows:** i.e., the bodies of Hermione and Mamillius.

<hr/>

III.iii. Antigonus leaves the baby girl in deserted country near the Bohemian coast. A bear frightens him from the scene just before a shepherd comes by and finds the child. The shepherd's son shortly appears and reports having seen a ship swallowed up by the sea and the mangling of Antigonus by a bear. The two shepherds wonder at the rich cloth in which the baby is wrapped and congratulate themselves on finding a hoard of treasure with the child. Delighted at their good fortune, the son goes off to bury whatever may remain of Antigonus.

<hr/>

1. **perfect:** certain.

3. **deserts of Bohemia:** Shakespeare merely followed his source, Greene's *Pandosto,* in giving a sea-coast to Bohemia.

Of what you should forget. Now, good my Liege,
Sir, royal sir, forgive a foolish woman. 250
The love I bore your queen—lo, fool again!
I'll speak of her no more, nor of your children:
I'll not remember you of my own lord,
Who is lost too. Take your patience to you,
And I'll say nothing. 255
 Leon.   Thou didst speak but well
When most the truth; which I receive much better
Than to be pitied of thee. Prithee, bring me
To the dead bodies of my queen and son.
One grave shall be for both. Upon them shall 260
The causes of their death appear, unto
Our shame perpetual. Once a day I'll visit
The chapel where they lie, and tears shed there
Shall be my recreation. So long as nature
Will bear up with this exercise, so long 265
I daily vow to use it. Come and lead me
To these sorrows.

        Exeunt.

Scene III. [Bohemia. A desert country near the sea.]

 Enter Antigonus [with] a Babe and a Mariner.

 Ant. Thou art perfect, then, our ship hath touched
  upon
The deserts of Bohemia?
 Mar.   Ay, my lord; and fear

6. **In my conscience:** I sincerely believe.

26-7. **of like sorrow,/ So filled and so becoming:** so full of becoming sorrow.

31. **Became two spouts:** gushed tears.

We have landed in ill time. The skies look grimly   5
And threaten present blusters. In my conscience,
The Heavens with that we have in hand are angry
And frown upon's.

   Ant. Their sacred wills be done! Go, get aboard;
Look to thy bark. I'll not be long before   10
I call upon thee.

   Mar. Make your best haste, and go not
Too far i' the land: 'tis like to be loud weather;
Besides, this place is famous for the creatures
Of prey that keep upon't.   15

   Ant.   Go thou away;
I'll follow instantly.

   Mar.   I am glad at heart
To be so rid o' the business.   *Exit.*

   Ant.   Come, poor babe.   20
I have heard, but not believed, the spirits o' the dead
May walk again. If such thing be, thy mother
Appeared to me last night, for ne'er was dream
So like a waking. To me comes a creature,
Sometimes her head on one side, some another: 25
I never saw a vessel of like sorrow,
So filled and so becoming. In pure white robes,
Like very sanctity, she did approach
My cabin where I lay; thrice bowed before me,
And, gasping to begin some speech, her eyes   30
Became two spouts. The fury spent, anon
Did this break from her: "Good Antigonus,
Since fate, against thy better disposition,
Hath made thy person for the thrower-out
Of my poor babe, according to thine oath,   35

37. **for:** because.

44. **toys:** trifles.

46. **squared:** ruled.

52. **character:** written statement of the child's parentage; **these:** gold and jewels.

53-4. **both breed thee . . . ,/ And still rest thine:** be sufficient to pay for your upbringing, with something left over.

56. **loss:** destruction.

Places remote enough are in Bohemia;
There weep and leave it crying; and, for the babe
Is counted lost forever, Perdita,
I prithee, call't. For this ungentle business,
Put on thee by my lord, thou ne'er shalt see   40
Thy wife Paulina more." And so, with shrieks,
She melted into air. Affrighted much,
I did in time collect myself and thought
This was so and no slumber. Dreams are toys:
Yet for this once, yea, superstitiously,   45
I will be squared by this. I do believe
Hermione hath suffered death; and that
Apollo would, this being indeed the issue
Of King Polixenes, it should here be laid,
Either for life or death, upon the earth   50
Of its right father. Blossom, speed thee well!
There lie, and there thy character: there these;
Which may, if fortune please, both breed thee, pretty,
And still rest thine. The storm begins. Poor wretch,
That for thy mother's fault art thus exposed   55
To loss and what may follow! Weep I cannot,
But my heart bleeds; and most accursed am I
To be by oath enjoined to this. Farewell!
The day frowns more and more. Thou'rt like to have
A lullaby too rough. I never saw   60
The heavens so dim by day. A savage clamor!
Well may I get aboard! This is the chase:
I am gone forever.   *Exit, pursued by a bear.*

[*Enter a Shepherd.*]

67. **the ancientry:** their elders.
75. **barne:** child; **child:** girl.
76. **scape:** escapade.
78-9. **stair work, . . . trunk work, . . . behind-door work:** i.e., the result of a love affair carried on by secret meetings.
85. **on:** of.

Shep. I would there were no age between ten and
three-and-twenty, or that youth would sleep out the 65
rest; for there is nothing in the between but getting
wenches with child, wronging the ancientry, stealing,
fighting—Hark you now! Would any but these boiled-
brains of nineteen and two-and-twenty hunt this
weather? They have scared away two of my best 70
sheep, which I fear the wolf will sooner find than the
master. If anywhere I have them, 'tis by the seaside,
browsing of ivy. Good luck, and't be Thy will! what
have we here? Mercy on's, a barne, a very pretty
barne! A boy **or a** child, I wonder? A pretty one, a 75
very pretty one: sure, some scape! Though I am not
bookish, yet I can read waiting gentlewoman in the
scape. This has been some stair work, some trunk
work, some behind-door work. They were warmer
that got this than the poor thing is here. I'll take it up 80
for pity; yet I'll tarry till my son come. He hallooed
but even now. Whoa, ho, hoa!

Enter Clown.

Clo. Hilloa, loa!
Shep. What, art so near? If thou'lt see a thing to
talk on when thou art dead and rotten, come hither. 85
What ailst thou, man?
Clo. I have seen two such sights, by sea and by
land! But I am not to say it is a sea, for it is now the
sky: betwixt the firmament and it you cannot thrust a
bodkin's point. 90

97. **yest:** foam.

98. **land service:** activity on land.

102. **flapdragoned it:** swallowed it as though it were a tidbit. A party game called "flapdragon" involved swallowing raisins from a bowl of flaming punch.

116. **Heavy:** sad; sorrowful.

119. **bearing cloth:** a covering in which the child was wrapped to be carried to baptism.

Shep. Why, boy, how is it?

Clo. I would you did but see how it chafes, how it
rages, how it takes up the shore! But that's not to the
point. Oh, the most piteous cry of the poor souls!
sometimes to see 'em, and not to see 'em. Now the   95
ship boring the moon with her mainmast, and anon
swallowed with yest and froth, as you'ld thrust a cork
into a hogshead. And then for the land service, to see
how the bear tore out his shoulder bone; how he
cried to me for help and said his name was Antigonus,   100
a nobleman. But to make an end of the ship, to see
how the sea flapdragoned it: but, first, how the poor
souls roared and the sea mocked them; and how the
poor gentleman roared and the bear mocked him,
both roaring louder than the sea or weather.   105

Shep. Name of mercy, when was this, boy?

Clo. Now, now! I have not winked since I saw
these sights. The men are not yet cold under water,
nor the bear half dined on the gentleman: he's at it
now.   110

Shep. Would I had been by, to have helped the old
man!

Clo. I would you had been by the ship side, to
have helped her: there your charity would have
lacked footing.   115

Shep. Heavy matters! heavy matters! But look thee
here, boy. Now bless thyself: thou mettst with things
dying, I with things newborn. Here's a sight for thee.
Look thee, a bearing cloth for a squire's child! Look
thee here: take up, take up, boy; open't. So let's see.   120

124. **well to live:** well-to-do.

127. **Up with't:** put it away; **close:** secret; **next:** nearest; shortest.

133. **curst:** vicious.

141-42. **we'll do good deeds on't:** an allusion to the proverb "The better the day, the better the deed."

It was told me I should be rich by the fairies. This is some changeling: open't. What's within, boy?

Clo. You're a made old man. If the sins of your youth are forgiven you, you're well to live. Gold! all gold!   125

Shep. This is fairy gold, boy, and 'twill prove so. Up with't, keep it close. Home, home, the next way. We are lucky, boy; and to be so still requires nothing but secrecy. Let my sheep go! Come, good boy, the next way home.   130

Clo. Go you the next way with your findings. I'll go see if the bear be gone from the gentleman and how much he hath eaten. They are never curst but when they are hungry. If there be any of him left, I'll bury it.   135

Shep. That's a good deed. If thou mayest discern by that which is left of him what he is, fetch me to the sight of him.

Clo. Marry, will I; and you shall help to put him i' the ground.   140

Shep. 'Tis a lucky day, boy, and we'll do good deeds on't.

Exeunt.

THE WINTER'S TALE

ACT IV

IV.i. Time, the Chorus, reports the lapse of sixteen years and a change of scene to Bohemia, where the King's son, Florizel, will be seen with Perdita, the shepherd's daughter.

‖‖‖‖‖‖‖‖‖‖‖‖‖‖‖‖‖‖‖‖‖‖‖‖

1. **try all:** "Time tries all things" was a proverbial idea.

4. **in the name of:** with the authority of.

10. **pass:** pass for.

12. **received:** accepted as proper.

14-6. **make stale/ The glistering of this present, as my tale/ Now seems to it:** make the shining present as outdated as the tale I tell of past happenings.

18. **As:** as if.

19. **fond:** foolish.

Time. From G. A. Gilio, *Topica poetica* (1580).

ACT IV

Scene I

Enter Time, the Chorus.

Time. I, that please some, try all, both joy and
   terror
Of good and bad, that makes and unfolds error,
Now take upon me, in the name of Time,
To use my wings. Impute it not a crime   5
To me or my swift passage that I slide
O'er sixteen years and leave the growth untried
Of that wide gap, since it is in my pow'r
To o'erthrow law and in one self-born hour
To plant and o'erwhelm custom. Let me pass   10
The same I am, ere ancient'st order was
Or what is now received. I witness to
The times that brought them in; so shall I do
To the freshest things now reigning, and make stale
The glistering of this present, as my tale   15
Now seems to it. Your patience this allowing,
I turn my glass and give my scene such growing
As you had slept between. Leontes leaving,
The effects of his fond jealousies so grieving
That he shuts up himself, imagine me,   20

24. **pace:** proceed.

26. **Equal with wond'ring:** matching the admiration she inspires.

27. **list not prophesy:** do not care to prophesy.

30. **adheres:** belongs.

31. **argument:** theme.

33. **yet:** yet allow (admit).

‖‖‖‖‖‖‖‖‖‖‖‖‖‖‖‖‖‖‖‖‖‖‖‖‖‖‖‖‖‖‖‖‖‖‖‖‖‖

IV.ii. Camillo begs Polixenes to allow him to return to Sicilia, but Polixenes, unable to do without Camillo's services, denies his request. He asks about the activities of Prince Florizel. The Prince has been much absent from the Court. Polixenes has heard that he is often at a shepherd's humble home and suspects that the shepherd's daughter is the attraction. He suggests that Camillo accompany him to question the shepherd.

‖‖‖‖‖‖‖‖‖‖‖‖‖‖‖‖‖‖‖‖‖‖‖‖‖‖‖‖‖‖

2. **'Tis a sickness:** i.e., it distresses Polixenes.

5. **been aired abroad:** breathed foreign air.

8. **allay:** easement; **o'erween:** presume.

Gentle spectators, that I now may be
In fair Bohemia; and remember well,
I mentioned a son o' the King's, which Florizel
I now name to you; and with speed so pace
To speak of Perdita, now grown in grace   25
Equal with wond'ring. What of her ensues
I list not prophesy; but let Time's news
Be known when 'tis brought forth. A shepherd's
      daughter,
And what to her adheres, which follows after,   30
Is the argument of Time. Of this allow,
If ever you have spent time worse ere now;
If never, yet that Time himself doth say
He wishes earnestly you never may.

                                        Exit.

Scene II. [Bohemia. The palace of Polixenes.]

Enter Polixenes and Camillo.

Pol. I pray thee, good Camillo, be no more impor-
tunate. 'Tis a sickness denying thee anything; a death
to grant this.

Cam. It is fifteen years since I saw my country.
Though I have for the most part been aired abroad, I   5
desire to lay my bones there. Besides, the penitent
King, my master, hath sent for me; to whose feeling
sorrows I might be some allay, or I o'erween to think
so, which is another spur to my departure.

Pol. As thou lovest me, Camillo, wipe not out the   10

13. **want:** lack.

14. **made me businesses:** undertaken affairs of business for me.

27. **gracious:** virtuous.

28. **approved:** demonstrated.

31. **missingly noted:** observed from missing his presence.

34. **considered so much:** believed as much.

38. **homely:** plain; uncultivated.

40. **unspeakable estate:** wealth beyond description.

rest of thy services by leaving me now. The need I
have of thee thine own goodness hath made; better
not to have had thee than thus to want thee. Thou,
having made me businesses, which none without thee
can sufficiently manage, must either stay to execute   15
them thyself, or take away with thee the very services
thou hast done; which if I have not enough considered, as too much I cannot, to be more thankful to
thee shall be my study; and my profit therein, the
heaping friendships. Of that fatal country, Sicilia,   20
prithee speak no more; whose very naming punishes
me with the remembrance of that penitent, as thou
callst him, and reconciled King, my brother; whose
loss of his most precious queen and children are even
now to be afresh lamented. Say to me, when sawst   25
thou the Prince Florizel, my son? Kings are no less
unhappy, their issue not being gracious, than they are
in losing them when they have approved their virtues.

    Cam. Sir, it is three days since I saw the Prince.
What his happier affairs may be are to me unknown;   30
but I have missingly noted he is of late much retired
from Court and is less frequent to his princely exer-
cises than formerly he hath appeared.

    Pol. I have considered so much, Camillo, and with
some care, so far that I have eyes under my service   35
which look upon his removedness; from whom I have
this intelligence, that he is seldom from the house of a
most homely shepherd; a man, they say, that from
very nothing and beyond the imagination of his
neighbors is grown into an unspeakable estate.   40

    Cam. I have heard, sir, of such a man, who hath a

42. note: reputation; fame.

42-4. The report of her is extended more than can be thought to begin from such a cottage: her praise goes beyond what can be believed of one so humbly born.

48. question: conversation.

IV.iii. Autolycus, a cheerful rogue, meets the shepherd's son on his way to purchase supplies for a sheep-shearing feast. Pretending to need help, Autolycus manages to rob the shepherd of his money. He resolves to attend the sheep shearing, which promises to yield him further profits.

---

1. peer: appear.

2. doxy: beggar's mate; slut.

4. winter's pale: cheeks paled by the darkness of winter.

8. an: on.

Battus is changed to stone by Mercury after revealing to Apollo where Mercury took his cattle. From Gabriele Simeoni, *Le vita et Metamorfoseo d'Ovidio* (1559).

(See IV.iii. for line 27.)

daughter of most rare note. The report of her is extended more than can be thought to begin from such
a cottage.

Pol. That's likewise part of my intelligence; but, I   45
fear, the angle that plucks our son thither. Thou shalt
accompany us to the place, where we will, not appearing what we are, have some question with the
shepherd; from whose simplicity I think it is not
uneasy to get the cause of my son's resort thither.   50
Prithee, be my present partner in this business and
lay aside the thoughts of Sicilia.

Cam. I willingly obey your command.

Pol. My best Camillo! We must disguise ourselves.
                                        Exeunt.

Scene III. [Bohemia. A road near the shepherd's
                        cottage.]

Enter Autolycus, singing.

Aut. When daffodils begin to peer,
            With heigh! the doxy over the dale,
        Why, then comes in the sweet o' the year;
            For the red blood reigns in the winter's pale.

The white sheet bleaching on the hedge,   5
            With heigh! the sweet birds, oh, how they
                sing!
        Doth set my pugging tooth an edge;
            For a quart of ale is a dish for a king.

13. **aunts:** sexual partners; paramours.

16. **three-pile:** velvet of triple thickness, the most expensive variety.

22. **budget:** bag, in which he carried his tools.

23. **my account:** i.e., his tale that he is a tinker pursuing his trade. Failing to provide himself with a useful occupation could mean punishment in the stocks, or worse, for vagrancy.

25. **kite:** a bird known to use pieces of cloth in building its nests.

27. **littered under Mercury:** born under the sign of Mercury. Ovid, *Metamorphoses,* bk. xi, tells how Mercury took advantage of Chione and the product of their love was named Autolycus, who became noted for his dishonesty. Mercury, who stole Apollo's cattle while still a babe, was the patron saint of thieves and liars.

28. **unconsidered:** unvalued, or, perhaps, unwatched; **die and drab:** gambling and women.

28-9. **purchased:** acquired.

29. **caparison:** trappings, i.e., rags. Autolycus has beggared himself, in other words, by indulging his vices.

29-30. **my revenue is the silly cheat:** my living comes from petty fraud.

30-1. **Gallows and knock are too powerful on the highway:** i.e., the penalties, hanging and beating respectively, deter him from highway robbery or downright begging.

32. **sleep out the thought of it:** forbear to think of it (eternity).

34. **every 'leven wether tods:** every eleven wethers (male sheep) produce a tod of wool (about 28 pounds).

62

The lark, that tirra-lyra chants,   10
    With heigh! with heigh! the thrush and the
        jay,
Are summer songs for me and my aunts,
    While we lie tumbling in the hay.

I have served Prince Florizel and in my time wore   15
three-pile; but now I am out of service:

But shall I go mourn for that, my dear?
    The pale moon shines by night:
And when I wander here and there.
    I then do most go right.   20

If tinkers may have leave to live,
    And bear the sow-skin budget,
Then my account I well may give,
    And in the stocks avouch it.

My traffic is sheets; when the kite builds, look to lesser   25
linen. My father named me Autolycus, who being, as
I am, littered under Mercury, was likewise a snapper-
up of unconsidered trifles. With die and drab I purchased this caparison, and my revenue is the silly
cheat. Gallows and knock are too powerful on the   30
highway: beating and hanging are terrors to me. For
the life to come, I sleep out the thought of it. A prize!
a prize!

Enter Clown.

Clo. Let me see: every 'leven wether tods; every

37. **springe:** snare; **cock:** woodcock; fool.

38. **compters:** tokens, used in place of coins for reckoning accounts.

42. **lays it on:** provides lavishly.

44. **three-man songmen:** singers of songs in three or more parts.

45. **means:** middle voices.

47. **warden:** variety of pear.

48. **out of my note:** not on my list.

49. **race:** root.

50-1. **raisins o' the sun:** raisins made by drying grapes in the sun rather than by artificial means.

Mercury and Chione; birth of Autolycus. From Gabriele Simeoni, *Le vita et Metamorfoseo d'Ovidio* (1559). (See IV.iii. 26–7.)

tod yields pound and odd shilling; fifteen hundred   35
shorn, what comes the wool to?

Aut. [*Aside*] If the springe hold, the cock's mine.

Clo. I cannot do't without compters. Let me see:
what am I to buy for our sheep-shearing feast? Three
pound of sugar; five pound of currants; rice—what   40
will this sister of mine do with rice? But my father
hath made her mistress of the feast, and she lays it on.
She hath made me four-and-twenty nosegays for the
shearers, three-man songmen all, and very good ones;
but they are most of them means and basses; but one   45
Puritan amongst them, and he sings psalms to horn-
pipes. I must have saffron to color the warden pies;
mace; dates—none, that's out of my note—nutmegs,
seven; a race or two of ginger, but that I may beg;
four pound of prunes, and as many of raisins o' the   50
sun.

Aut. Oh, that ever I was born!

[*Groveling on the ground.*]

Clo. I' the name of me—

Aut. Oh, help me, help me! Pluck but off these
rags; and then, death, death!   55

Clo. Alack, poor soul! thou hast need of more rags
to lay on thee, rather than have these off.

Aut. O sir, the loathsomeness of them offend me
more than the stripes I have received, which are
mighty ones and millions.   60

Clo. Alas, poor man! a million of beating may come
to a great matter.

Aut. I am robbed, sir, and beaten; my money and

77. **Softly:** gently.

89. **troll-my-dames:** a game involving balls which were to be rolled into nine holes. The fellow operated the game at markets and fairs.

Catching woodcocks in springes. From H. Parrot,
Laquei ridiculosi (1613). (See IV.iii. 37.)

apparel ta'en from me, and these detestable things put
upon me. 65

Clo. What, by a horseman, or a footman?

Aut. A footman, sweet sir, a footman.

Clo. Indeed, he should be a footman, by the garments he has left with thee. If this be a horseman's
coat, it hath seen very hot service. Lend me thy hand, 70
I'll help thee. Come, lend me thy hand.

[*Helping him up.*]

Aut. O good sir, tenderly, O!

Clo. Alas, poor soul!

Aut. O good sir, softly, good sir! I fear, sir, my
shoulder blade is out. 75

Clo. How now! canst stand?

Aut. [*Picking his pocket*] Softly, dear sir; good sir,
softly. You ha' done me a charitable office.

Clo. Dost lack any money? I have a little money
for thee. 80

Aut. No, good sweet sir; no, I beseech you, sir. I
have a kinsman not past three-quarters of a mile
hence, unto whom I was going. I shall there have
money, or anything I want. Offer me no money, I pray
you; that kills my heart. 85

Clo. What manner of fellow was he that robbed
you?

Aut. A fellow, sir, that I have known to go about
with troll-my-dames. I knew him once a servant of
the Prince. I cannot tell, good sir, for which of his 90
virtues it was, but he was certainly whipped out of
the court.

Clo. His vices, you would say. There's no virtue

95. **no more but abide:** barely linger.

97. **ape bearer:** i.e., he traveled with a monkey, like the modern organ grinder.

98. **compassed:** procured; **motion:** puppet show.

103. **Prig:** a cant term for both "tinker" and "thief."

108. **big:** threatening.

117. **bring:** escort.

123. **cheat:** fraud.

123-24. **bring out:** lead to.

A tinker with a budget on his back. From a
seventeenth-century broadside ballad. (See IV.iii. 21–2.)

whipped out of the court: they cherish it to make it
stay there; and yet it will no more but abide.   95

Aut. Vices I would say, sir. I know this man well.
He hath been since an ape bearer; then a process
server, a bailiff; then he compassed a motion of the
Prodigal Son and married a tinker's wife within a
mile where my land and living lies; and, having flown   100
over many knavish professions, he settled only in
rogue. Some call him Autolycus.

Clo. Out upon him! Prig, for my life, prig. He
haunts wakes, fairs, and bear-baitings.

Aut. Very true, sir; he, sir, he. That's the rogue that 105
put me into this apparel.

Clo. Not a more cowardly rogue in all Bohemia. If
you had but looked big and spit at him, he'ld have
run.

Aut. I must confess to you, sir, I am no fighter. I am   110
false of heart that way; and that he knew, I warrant
him.

Clo. How do you now?

Aut. Sweet sir, much better than I was: I can stand
and walk. I will even take my leave of you and pace   115
softly toward my kinsman's.

Clo. Shall I bring thee on the way?

Aut. No, good-faced sir; no, sweet sir.

Clo. Then fare thee well. I must go buy spices for
our sheep shearing.   *Exit [Clown].*   120

Aut. Prosper you, sweet sir! Your purse is not hot
enough to purchase your spice. I'll be with you at
your sheep shearing too. If I make not this cheat bring

124. **prove sheep:** i.e., ripe for shearing.

125. **unrolled:** removed from the catalogue of rogues.

127. **hent:** make use of.

||||||||||||||||||||||||||||||||||||||||||||||||||||||

IV.iv. Florizel, disguised as a shepherd, has taken the name Doricles in order to woo Perdita, the shepherd's daughter. Polixenes and Camillo, in disguise, attend the sheep shearing. Although charmed by the grace and beauty of Perdita, the King reveals himself and threatens her and her father for entrapping his son. The despairing Florizel plans to embark with Perdita on a ship that he has ready, and Camillo counsels the pair to seek the hospitality of Leontes in Sicilia. The latter, penitent for his wrong to Polixenes, will make amends by welcoming his son. Camillo hopes that if he informs Polixenes of Florizel's flight, the King will pursue him and take Camillo to Sicilia too. The shepherd and his son seek the King to tell him that Perdita is a changeling and not the shepherd's daughter. They meet Autolycus, who entices them aboard Florizel's ship.

||||||||||||||||||||||||||||||||||||||||||||||||||||||

1. **weeds:** garments.

2-3. **Flora,/ Peering in April's front:** the Roman goddess of flowers, appearing with a spring-like face.

7. **extremes:** extravagances.

9. **gracious mark o' the land:** i.e., graced object of everyone's regard.

10. **swain's wearing:** rustic's (shepherd's) attire.

11. **pranked up:** decked out.

13. **Digest it with a custom:** accept it because they are used to it.

out another and the shearers prove sheep, let me be
unrolled and my name put in the book of virtue! 125

Song.

Jog on, jog on, the footpath way,
    And merrily hent the stile-a.
A merry heart goes all the day,
    Your sad tires in a mile-a.

Exit.

Scene IV. [Bohemia. The shepherd's cottage.]

Enter Florizel and Perdita.

Flo. These your unusual weeds to each part of you
Does give a life: no shepherdess, but Flora,
Peering in April's front. This your sheep shearing
Is as a meeting of the petty gods,
And you the queen on't. 5
   Per.   Sir, my gracious lord,
To chide at your extremes it not becomes me:
Oh, pardon, that I name them! Your high self,
The gracious mark o' the land, you have obscured
With a swain's wearing, and me, poor lowly maid, 10
Most goddess-like pranked up. But that our feasts
In every mess have folly, and the feeders
Digest it with a custom, I should blush
To see you so attired, swoon, I think,
To show myself a glass. 15
   Flo.   I bless the time

26. **flaunts:** finery.

31-2. **Jupiter/ Became a bull:** in order to abduct Europa.

32-3. **Neptune/ A ram:** for love of Theophane.

34. **Apollo, a poor humble swain:** on several occasions.

When my good falcon made her flight across
Thy father's ground.
   Per.   Now Jove afford you cause!
To me the difference forges dread; your greatness   20
Hath not been used to fear. Even now I tremble
To think your father, by some accident,
Should pass this way as you did. O the Fates!
How would he look, to see his work, so noble,
Vilely bound up? What would he say? Or how   25
Should I, in these my borrowed flaunts, behold
The sternness of his presence?
   Flo.   Apprehend
Nothing but jollity. The gods themselves,
Humbling their deities to love, have taken   30
The shapes of beasts upon them. Jupiter
Became a bull and bellowed; the green Neptune
A ram and bleated; and the fire-robed god,
Golden Apollo, a poor humble swain,
As I seem now. Their transformations   35
Were never for a piece of beauty rarer,
Nor in a way so chaste, since my desires
Run not before mine honor, nor my lusts
Burn hotter than my faith.
   Per.   O, but, sir,   40
Your resolution cannot hold when 'tis
Opposed, as it must be, by the pow'r of the King:
One of these two must be necessities,
Which then will speak, that you must change this
    purpose,   45
Or I my life.
   Flo.   Thou dearest Perdita,

48. **forced:** labored; grievous.
49. **Or:** either.
62. **Address:** prepare; **sprightly:** cheerfully.
65. **pantler:** server of food from the pantry.
66. **dame:** mistress.

Cotswold shepherds dancing. From Michael Drayton,
Polyolbion (1612).

With these forced thoughts, I prithee, darken not
The mirth o' the feast. Or I'll be thine, my fair,
Or not my father's. For I cannot be   50
Mine own, nor anything to any, if
I be not thine. To this I am most constant,
Though destiny say no. Be merry, gentle;
Strangle such thoughts as these with anything
That you behold the while. Your guests are coming: 55
Lift up your countenance, as it were the day
Of celebration of that nuptial which
We two have sworn shall come.
  Per.   O Lady Fortune,
Stand you auspicious!   60
  Flo.   See, your guests approach.
Address yourself to entertain them sprightly,
And let's be red with mirth.

[*Enter Shepherd, Clown, Mopsa, Dorcas, and others,
      with Polixenes and Camillo disguised.*]

  Shep. Fie, daughter! when my old wife lived, upon
This day she was both pantler, butler, cook,   65
Both dame and servant; welcomed all, served all;
Would sing her song and dance her turn; now here,
At upper end o' the table, now i' the middle;
On his shoulder and his; her face o' fire
With labor, and the thing she took to quench it   70
She would to each one sip. You are retired,
As if you were a feasted one and not
The hostess of the meeting. Pray you, bid
These unknown friends to's welcome; for it is

85. **rosemary and rue:** rosemary signified "re-membrance"; **rue** was also known as "herb of grace," hence Perdita's mention of **grace** and **remembrance** in line 87.

86. **Seeming and savor:** i.e., they remain fresh in color and scent.

95. **gillyvors:** gillyflowers, or clove pinks.

96. **Nature's bastards:** apparently because flowers of different colors would grow from the seed of one variety.

102. **piedness:** streakedness.

2 Caryophyllus multiplex.
The double Cloue Gilloflower.

Gillyflowers. From John Gerard, *Herbal* (1597).

A way to make us better friends, more known.   75
Come, quench your blushes and present yourself
That which you are, mistress o' the feast. Come on,
And bid us welcome to your sheep shearing,
As your good flock shall prosper.
   Per.   Sir, welcome.   80
It is my father's will I should take on me
The hostess-ship o' the day. [*To Camillo*] You're wel-
   come, sir.
Give me those flow'rs there, Dorcas. Reverend sirs,
For you there's rosemary and rue: these keep   85
Seeming and savor all the winter long.
Grace and remembrance be to you both,
And welcome to our shearing!
   Pol.   Shepherdess,
A fair one are you, well you fit our ages   90
With flow'rs of winter.
   Per.   Sir, the year growing ancient,
Not yet on summer's death nor on the birth
Of trembling winter, the fairest flow'rs o' the season
Are our carnations and streaked gillyvors,   95
Which some call Nature's bastards. Of that kind
Our rustic garden's barren, and I care not
To get slips of them.
   Pol.   Wherefore, gentle maiden,
Do you neglect them?   100
   Per.   For I have heard it said
There is an art which in their piedness shares
With great creating Nature.
   Pol.   Say there be;
Yet nature is made better by no mean   105

109. **scion:** slip; shoot.

112. **mend:** improve upon.

118. **dibble:** a small tool used to make holes in which to plant seed.

124. **weeping:** dewy.

136. **Proserpina:** daughter of Ceres, stolen by Pluto, or Dis, and carried to his underground kingdom.

An emblem signifying a common idea of the period, that Art corrects Nature. The figure at the left is Mercury repairing a broken lute. From Geoffrey Whitney, *A Choice of Emblems* (1586).

But nature makes that mean. So, over that art
Which you say adds to nature, is an art
That nature makes. You see, sweet maid, we marry
A gentler scion to the wildest stock,
And make conceive a bark of baser kind   110
By bud of nobler race. This is an art
Which does mend nature, change it rather, but
The art itself is nature.

    Per.   So it is.

    Pol. Then make your garden rich in gillyvors,   115
And do not call them bastards.

    Per.   I'll not put
The dibble in earth to set one slip of them;
No more than were I painted I would wish
This youth should say 'twere well and only therefore   120
Desire to breed by me. Here's flow'rs for you;
Hot lavender, mints, savory, marjoram;
The marigold, that goes to bed wi' the sun
And with him rises weeping. These are flow'rs
Of middle summer, and I think they are given   125
To men of middle age. Y'are very welcome.

    Cam. I should leave grazing, were I of your flock,
And only live by gazing.

    Per.   Out, alas!
You'ld be so lean that blasts of January   130
Would blow you through and through. Now, my
    fair'st friend,
I would I had some flow'rs o' the spring that might
Become your time of day; and yours, and yours,
That wear upon your virgin branches yet   135
Your maidenheads growing. O Proserpina,

139. **take:** charm.

142. **Cytherea:** Venus.

142-44. **pale primroses,/ That die unmarried ere they can behold/ Bright Phoebus in his strength:** primroses, early spring flowers, that die before the sun has attained to summer heat, are compared with virgins with the characteristic illness known as greensickness, or chlorosis, a kind of anaemia. In folklore, girls who died of this anaemia were said to be changed to primroses.

150. **corse:** corpse.

153. **quick:** alive.

155. **Whitsun pastorals:** the May Day festivals celebrated beginning the seventh Sunday after Easter and including Morris dancers, etc.

158. **Still betters what is done:** is ever better than what you have done before.

165-68. **Each your doing,/ So singular in each particular,/ Crowns what you are doing in the present deeds,/ That all your acts are queens:** everything you do is characteristic of you in every detail, so that it renders your present action supreme and all your actions are superior to those of anyone else.

For the flow'rs now that, frighted, thou letst fall
From Dis's waggon! daffodils,
That come before the swallow dares and take
The winds of March with beauty; violets, dim,   140
But sweeter than the lids of Juno's eyes
Or Cytherea's breath; pale primroses,
That die unmarried ere they can behold
Bright Phoebus in his strength—a malady
Most incident to maids; bold oxlips and   145
The crown imperial; lilies of all kinds,
The flow'r-de-luce being one! Oh, these I lack,
To make you garlands of; and my sweet friend,
To strew him o'er and o'er!
    Flo.   What, like a corse?   150
    Per. No, like a bank for love to lie and play on;
Not like a corse; or if, not to be buried,
But quick and in mine arms. Come, take your flow'rs:
Methinks I play as I have seen them do
In Whitsun pastorals. Sure this robe of mine   155
Does change my disposition.
    Flo.   What you do
Still betters what is done. When you speak, sweet,
I'ld have you do it ever. When you sing,
I'ld have you buy and sell so, so give alms,   160
Pray so; and, for the ord'ring your affairs,
To sing them too. When you do dance, I wish you
A wave o' the sea, that you might ever do
Nothing but that; move still, still so,
And own no other function. Each your doing,   165
So singular in each particular,
Crowns what you are doing in the present deeds,

176. **skill:** reason.

178. **turtles:** turtledoves.

189-90. **Marry, garlic,/ To mend her kissing with:** yes, indeed, give her some garlic to sweeten her breath.

191. **in good time:** is that so!

192-93. **stand upon our manners:** are obliged to be polite.

Proserpina's abduction by Pluto. From Claude Menestrier, *L'art des emblemes* (1684). (See IV.iv. 136–38.)

That all your acts are queens.

Per.   O Doricles,
Your praises are too large: but that your youth,   170
And the true blood which peeps fairly through't,
Do plainly give you out an unstained shepherd,
With wisdom I might fear, my Doricles,
You wooed me the false way.

Flo.   I think you have   175
As little skill to fear as I have purpose
To put you to't. But come; our dance, I pray:
Your hand, my Perdita. So turtles pair
That never mean to part.

Per.   I'll swear for 'em.   180

Pol. This is the prettiest lowborn lass that ever
Ran on the greensward. Nothing she does or seems
But smacks of something greater than herself,
Too noble for this place.

Cam.   He tells her something   185
That makes her blood look out. Good sooth, she is
The queen of curds and cream.

Clo.   Come on, strike up!

Dor. Mopsa must be your mistress. Marry, garlic,
To mend her kissing with!   190

Mop.   Now, in good time!

Clo. Not a word, a word: we stand upon our
     manners.
Come, strike up!

         [*Music.*] *Here a dance of Shepherds and*
                         Shepherdesses.

Pol. Pray, good shepherd, what fair swain is this   195
Which dances with your daughter?

198. **feeding:** pasturage for sheep.

200. **sooth:** truth.

206. **featly:** gracefully.

212. **tabor:** a small drum.

214. **tell:** count.

217. **better:** more opportunely.

218-20. **doleful matter merrily set down, or a very pleasant thing indeed and sung lamentably:** these contradictory descriptions are typical of clownish humor.

222. **milliner:** a seller not of hats but of general haberdashery.

224. **burdens:** refrains.

Shep. They call him Doricles; and boasts himself
To have a worthy feeding; but I have it
Upon his own report and I believe it:
He looks like sooth. He says he loves my daughter: 200
I think so too; for never gazed the moon
Upon the water as he'll stand and read
As 'twere my daughter's eyes; and, to be plain,
I think there is not half a kiss to choose
Who loves another best.   205
     Pol.   She dances featly.
     Shep. So she does anything; though I report it
That should be silent. If young Doricles
Do light upon her, she shall bring him that
Which he not dreams of.   210

Enter Servant.

     Ser. O master, if you did but hear the peddler at
the door, you would never dance again after a tabor
and pipe; no, the bagpipe could not move you. He
sings several tunes faster than you'll tell money; he
utters them as he had eaten ballads and all men's ears   215
grew to his tunes.
     Clo. He could never come better: he shall come in.
I love a ballad but even too well, if it be doleful
matter merrily set down, or a very pleasant thing
indeed and sung lamentably.   220
     Ser. He hath songs for man or woman, of all sizes.
No milliner can so fit his customers with gloves. He
has the prettiest love songs for maids; so without
bawdry, which is strange; with such delicate burdens

225. **dildos:** common nonsense refrain words: **fadings:** another term for refrains.

227. **foul gap:** bawdy interlude.

231. **brave:** splendid.

232-33. **an admirable conceited fellow:** a fellow of admirable wit.

233. **unbraided:** fresh, rather than shopworn.

235. **points:** laces.

237. **inkles:** linen tape; **caddises:** ribbons.

239. **smock:** shirt, usually a feminine undergarment.

240. **sleevehand:** wrist edging; **work about the square on't:** embroidery on the bosom of it.

245. **You have of these peddlers:** i.e., there are some peddlers of this kind.

247. **go about:** attempt.

249. **Cypress:** a sheer black fabric, mainly used for mourning garments.

250. **sweet:** perfumed.

252. **Bugle:** made of bugles, small beads.

of dildos and fadings, "jump her and thump her"; 225
and where some stretch-mouthed rascal would, as it
were, mean mischief and break a foul gap into the
matter, he makes the maid to answer, "Whoop, do me
no harm, good man"; puts him off, slights him, with
"Whoop, do me no harm, good man." 230

Pol. This is a brave fellow.

Clo. Believe me, thou talkest of an admirable conceited fellow. Has he any unbraided wares?

Ser. He hath ribbons of all the colors i' the rain-
bow; points more than all the lawyers in Bohemia can 235
learnedly handle, though they come to him by the
gross; inkles, caddises, cambrics, lawns. Why, he sings
'em over as they were gods or goddesses: you would
think a smock were a she-angel, he so chants to the
sleevehand and the work about the square on't. 240

Clo. Prithee bring him in, and let him approach
singing.

Per. Forewarn him that he use no scurrilous words
in's tunes. [*Exit Servant.*]

Clo. You have of these peddlers that have more in 245
them than you'ld think, sister.

Per. Ay, good brother, or go about to think.

Enter Autolycus, singing.

Aut. Lawn as white as driven snow,
Cypress black as e'er was crow,
Gloves as sweet as damask roses, 250
Masks for faces, and for noses:
Bugle bracelet, necklace amber,

254. **coifs:** women's caps; **stomachers:** decorative central pieces for feminine bodices.

256. **poking sticks:** instruments similar to curling irons, used to pleat ruffs and cuffs.

265. **against:** before.

273. **plackets:** petticoats.

275. **kilnhole:** the fire hole of an oven, probably used for making malt.

277. **clamor:** silence, from the word "clamber," a term from bellringing, meaning to stop the noise of.

280. **tawdry lace:** a neckerchief, named after St. Audrey. Such neckwear originated at the annual St. Audrey's Fair held at Ely, but the term later came to be applied to cheap trinkets of various kinds.

281. **cozened:** cheated.

Perfume for a lady's chamber:
Golden coifs, and stomachers
For my lads, to give their dears: 255
Pins and poking sticks of steel.
What maids lack from head to heel:
Come buy of me, come: come buy, come buy!
Buy lads, or else your lasses cry:
Come buy!   260

Clo. If I were not in love with Mopsa, thou shouldst
take no money of me; but being enthralled as I am, it
will also be the bondage of certain ribbons and
gloves.

Mop. I was promised them against the feast; but 265
they come not too late now.

Dor. He hath promised you more than that, or there
be liars.

Mop. He hath paid you all he promised you. May
be, he has paid you more, which will shame you to 270
give him again.

Clo. Is there no manners left among maids? Will
they wear their plackets where they should bear their
faces? Is there not milking time, when you are going
to bed, or kilnhole, to whistle off these secrets, but 275
you must be tittle-tattling before all our guests? 'Tis
well they are whisp'ring: clamor your tongues, and
not a word more.

Mop. I have done. Come, you promised me a
tawdry lace and a pair of sweet gloves.   280

Clo. Have I not told thee how I was cozened by the
way and lost all my money?

284. **behooves:** obliges.
288. **charge:** value.
291. **o' life:** on my life.
295. **carbonadoed:** slashed and grilled.
303. **mo:** other.

An itinerant peddler. From Hartmann Schopper, *Panoplia* (1568).

Aut. And indeed, sir, there are cozeners abroad: therefore it behooves men to be wary.

Clo. Fear not thou, man, thou shalt lose nothing 285 here.

Aut. I hope so, sir; for I have about me many parcels of charge.

Clo. What hast here? Ballads?

Mop. Pray now, buy some. I love a ballad in print 290 o' life, for then we are sure they are true.

Aut. Here's one to a very doleful tune, how a usurer's wife was brought to bed of twenty money bags at a burden, and how she longed to eat adders' heads and toads carbonadoed. 295

Mop. Is it true, think you?

Aut. Very true, and but a month old.

Dor. Bless me from marrying a usurer!

Aut. Here's the midwife's name to't, one Mistress Taleporter, and five or six honest wives that were 300 present. Why should I carry lies abroad?

Mop. Pray you now, buy it.

Clo. Come on, lay it by: and let's first see mo ballads. We'll buy the other things anon.

Aut. Here's another ballad of a fish that appeared 305 upon the coast, on Wednesday the fourscore of April, forty thousand fathom above water, and sung this ballad against the hard hearts of maids. It was thought she was a woman and was turned into a cold fish for she would not exchange flesh with one that 310 loved her. The ballad is very pitiful and as true.

Dor. Is it true too, think you?

318. **passing:** surpassingly.
326. **Have at it with you:** let's get on with it.
335. **Or:** either.

Aut. Five justices' hands at it, and witnesses more
than my pack will hold.

Clo. Lay it by too: another.   315

Aut. This is a merry ballad, but a very pretty one.

Mop. Let's have some merry ones.

Aut. Why, this is a passing merry one and goes to
the tune of "Two maids wooing a man." There's
scarce a maid westward but she sings it: 'tis in 320
request, I can tell you.

Mop. We can both sing it. If thou'lt bear a part,
thou shalt hear; 'tis in three parts.

Dor. We had the tune on't a month ago.

Aut. I can bear my part; you must know 'tis my 325
occupation. Have at it with you.

Song.

Aut.	Get you hence, for I must go
	Where it fits not you to know.
Dor.	Whither?
Mop.	Oh, whither? 330
Dor.	Whither?
Mop.	It becomes thy oath full well,
	Thou to me thy secrets tell.
Dor.	Me too, let me go thither.
Mop.	Or thou goest to the grange or mill: 335
Dor.	If to either, thou dost ill.
Aut.	Neither.
Dor.	What, neither?
Aut.	Neither.
Dor.	Thou hast sworn my love to be. 340

343. **have this song out:** sing the song through.

344. **sad:** grave.

353. **toys:** trifles.

357. **utter:** sell.

361. **saltiers:** tumblers. The clown possibly has been told that the dancers represent satyrs and confuses the word with an old word for acrobats.

362. **gallimaufry:** hodgepodge; mixture.

Mop. Thou hast sworn it more to me:
        Then whither goest? Say, whither?
Clo. We'll have this song out anon by ourselves.
My father and the gentlemen are in sad talk, and we'll
not trouble them. Come, bring away thy pack after 345
me. Wenches, I'll buy for you both. Peddler, let's have
the first choice. Follow me, girls.

                        [*Exit with Dorcas and Mopsa.*]
Aut. And you shall pay well for 'em.

                                [*Follows singing.*]
        Will you buy any tape,
          Or lace for your cape,   350
      My dainty duck, my dear-a?
          Any silk, any thread,
          Any toys for your head,
      Of the new'st, and fin'st, fin'st wear-a?
          Come to the peddler: 355
          Money's a meddler
      That doth utter all men's ware-a.   *Exit.*

                    [*Enter Servant.*]

Ser. Master, there is three carters, three shepherds,
three neatherds, three swineherds, that have made
themselves all men of hair; they call themselves   360
saltiers, and they have a dance which the wenches say
is a gallimaufry of gambols, because they are not in't;
but they themselves are o' the mind, if it be not too
rough for some that know little but bowling, it will
please plentifully.   365
Shep. Away! we'll none on't. Here has been too

367. **homely:** uncouth.

373. **squire:** square; rule.

385. **handed:** took by the hand; pledged by hand-clasp.

389. **marted:** traded.

390. **Interpretation should abuse:** should choose to misunderstand.

391. **straited:** hard put to it.

392-93. **make a care/ Of happy holding her:** are anxious to keep her happy.

A satyr. From Jacopo Caviceo, *Libro del peregrino* (1526).

much homely foolery already. I know, sir, we weary
you.

Pol. You weary those that refresh us. Pray, let's see
these four threes of herdsmen.   370

Ser. One three of them, by their own report, sir,
hath danced before the King; and not the worst of the
three but jumps twelve foot and a half by the squire.

Shep. Leave your prating. Since these good men
are pleased, let them come in; but quickly now.   375

Ser. Why, they stay at door, sir.

> *Here a dance of twelve Satyrs.*
> [*They dance, and then exeunt.*]

Pol. [*Aside*] O father, you'll know more of that
hereafter.

[*To Camillo*] Is it not too far gone? 'Tis time to part
them.   380

He's simple and tells much. [*To Florizel*] How now,
fair shepherd!

Your heart is full of something that does take
Your mind from feasting. Sooth, when I was young
And handed love as you do, I was wont   385
To load my she with knacks. I would have ransacked
The peddler's silken treasury and have poured it
To her acceptance: you have let him go
And nothing marted with him. If your lass
Interpretation should abuse and call this   390
Your lack of love or bounty, you were straited
For a reply, at least if you make a care
Of happy holding her.

Flo. Old sir, I know
She prizes not such trifles as these are.   395

402. **fanned . . . bolted:** sifted.

405-6. **wash/ The hand was fair before:** make her hand, which was already white, even whiter in his comparisons.

406. **put you out:** broken your train of thought (by interruption).

415. **force and knowledge:** power of knowledge.

418-19. **Commend them and condemn them to her service/ Or to their own perdition:** offer them to her service or to their own utter destruction.

The gifts she looks from me are packed and locked
Up in my heart; which I have given already,
But not delivered. Oh, hear me breathe my life
Before this ancient sir, who, it should seem,
Hath sometime loved! I take thy hand, this hand,   400
As soft as dove's down and as white as it,
Or Ethiopian's tooth, or the fanned snow that's bolted
By the northern blasts twice o'er.
  Pol.   What follows this?
How prettily the young swain seems to wash   405
The hand was fair before! I have put you out;
But to your protestation: let me hear
What you profess.
  Flo.   Do, and be witness to't.
  Pol. And this my neighbor too?   410
  Flo.   And he, and more
Than he, and men, the earth, the heavens, and all:
That, were I crowned the most imperial monarch,
Thereof most worthy, were I the fairest youth
That ever made eye swerve, had force and knowledge 415
More than was ever man's, I would not prize them
Without her love; for her employ them all;
Commend them and condemn them to her service
Or to their own perdition.
  Pol.   Fairly offered.   420
  Cam. This shows a sound affection.
  Shep.   But, my daughter,
Say you the like to him?
  Per.   I cannot speak
So well, nothing so well; no, nor mean better.   425

426-27. **By the pattern of mine own thoughts I cut out/ The purity of his:** I imagine his sincerity to be identical with my own; our feelings are the same.

431. **portion:** dowry.

433. **I' the virtue of your daughter:** i.e., her virtue in itself can match his portion, but the shepherd cannot possibly offer a dowry in money that would do so.

435. **for your wonder:** to amaze you.

439. **Soft:** hold.

450. **dispute:** discuss; **estate:** condition.

452. **being childish:** as a child.

By the pattern of mine own thoughts I cut out
The purity of his.
    Shep.   Take hands, a bargain!
And, friends unknown, you shall bear witness to't.
I give my daughter to him and will make   430
Her portion equal his.
    Flo. Oh, that must be
I' the virtue of your daughter. One being dead,
I shall have more than you can dream of yet:
Enough then for your wonder. But, come on,   435
Contract us 'fore these witnesses.
    Shep.   Come, your hand;
And, daughter, yours.
    Pol.   Soft, swain, awhile, beseech you:
Have you a father?   440
    Flo.   I have; but what of him?
    Pol. Knows he of this?
    Flo. He neither does nor shall.
    Pol. Methinks a father
Is at the nuptial of his son a guest   445
That best becomes the table. Pray you once more,
Is not your father grown incapable
Of reasonable affairs? Is he not stupid
With age and alt'ring rheums? Can he speak? hear?
Know man from man? dispute his own estate?   450
Lies he not bedrid? and again does nothing
But what he did being childish?
    Flo.   No, good sir;
He has his health and ampler strength indeed
Than most have of his age.   455
    Pol.   By my white beard,

458-59. **Reason my son/ Should choose:** it is reasonable that my son should choose.

478. **affects:** fancies.

480. **fresh:** lovely.

481. **of force:** necessarily.

486. **fond:** foolish.

You offer him, if this be so, a wrong
Something unfilial. Reason my son
Should choose himself a wife, but as good reason
The father, all whose joy is nothing else   460
But fair posterity, should hold some counsel
In such a business.

Flo.   I yield all this;
But for some other reasons, my grave sir,
Which 'tis not fit you know, I not acquaint   465
My father of this business.

Pol.   Let him know't.

Flo. He shall not.

Pol.   Prithee, let him.

Flo.   No, he must not.   470

Shep. Let him, my son. He shall not need to grieve
At knowing of thy choice.

Flo.   Come, come, he must not.
Mark our contract.

Pol.   Mark your divorce, young sir,   475
          [*Discovering himself.*]
Whom son I dare not call; thou art too base
To be acknowledged. Thou, a scepter's heir,
That thus affects a sheephook! Thou old traitor,
I am sorry that by hanging thee I can
But shorten thy life one week. And thou, fresh piece   480
Of excellent witchcraft, who of force must know
The royal fool thou copest with—

Shep.   Oh, my heart!

Pol. I'll have thy beauty scratched with briars and
          made   485
More homely than thy state.—For thee, fond boy,

488. **knack:** knickknack; trifle.

491. **Far:** farther; **Deucalion:** in Greek mythology Deucalion and his wife, Pyrrha, escaped a flood sent by Zeus to destroy the earth but were able with the god's help to repeople the land with men transformed from stone. A kinship traced back to Deucalion would thus be very remote indeed.

492. **churl:** peasant.

496. **but for our honor therein:** except for the honor he derives from us.

498. **rural latches:** rustic embraces.

Deucalion, after the flood, creates new men. From Lodovico Dolce, *Le trasformationi* (1570).

If I may ever know thou dost but sigh
That thou no more shalt see this knack, as never
I mean thou shalt, we'll bar thee from succession;
Not hold thee of our blood, no, not our kin,   490
Far than Deucalion off. Mark thou my words.
Follow us to the court.—Thou churl, for this time,
Though full of our displeasure, yet we free thee
From the dead blow of it.—And you, enchantment—
Worthy enough a herdsman; yea, him too,   495
That makes himself, but for our honor therein,
Unworthy thee—if ever henceforth thou
These rural latches to his entrance open,
Or hoop his body more with thy embraces,
I will devise a death as cruel for thee   500
As thou art tender to't.   *Exit.*
   Per.   Even here undone!
I was not much afeard; for once or twice
I was about to speak and tell him plainly,
The selfsame sun that shines upon his court   505
Hides not his visage from our cottage but
Looks on alike. [*To Florizel*] Will't please you, sir,
    be gone?
I told you what would come of this. Beseech you,
Of your own state take care. This dream of mine—   510
Being now awake, I'll queen it no inch farther,
But milk my ewes and weep.
   Cam.   Why, how now, father!
Speak ere thou diest.
   Shep.   I cannot speak, nor think,   515
Nor dare to know that which I know. [*To Florizel*] O
    sir!

Bredon Hill

A shepherd's feast. From Michael Drayton, *Polyolbion* (1612).

You have undone a man of fourscore three,
That thought to fill his grave in quiet; yea,
To die upon the bed my father died,   520
To lie close by his honest bones: but now
Some hangman must put on my shroud and lay me
Where no priest shovels in dust. [*To Perdita*] O
    cursed wretch,
That knewst this was the Prince and wouldst ad-   525
    venture
To mingle faith with him! Undone! undone!
If I might die within this hour, I have lived
To die when I desire.   *Exit.*
   Flo.   Why look you so upon me?   530
I am but sorry, not afeard; delayed,
But nothing altered. What I was, I am;
More straining on for plucking back, not following
My leash unwillingly.
   Cam.   Gracious my lord,   535
You know your father's temper. At this time
He will allow no speech, which I do guess
You do not purpose to him; and as hardly
Will he endure your sight as yet, I fear.
Then, till the fury of His Highness settle,   540
Come not before him.
   Flo.   I not purpose it.
I think, Camillo?
   Cam.   Even he, my lord.
   Per. How often have I told you 'twould be thus!   545
How often said my dignity would last
But till 'twere known!
   Flo.   It cannot fail but by

552-53. **I/ Am heir to my affection:** my love shall be my sole possession.

554. **Be advised:** take counsel (and change your mind).

555. **fancy:** love.

555-56. **If my reason/ Will thereto be obedient, I have reason:** if I can make my reason serve my love (make possible its realization), I shall be sane.

561. **honesty:** honorable behavior.

570. **passion:** grief.

571. **Tug:** contend.

572. **deliver:** report.

578. **Concern me the reporting:** be to my advantage to report.

The violation of my faith; and then
Let nature crush the sides o' the earth together   550
And mar the seeds within! Lift up thy looks.
From my succession wipe me, father, I
Am heir to my affection.
    Cam.   Be advised.
    Flo. I am, and by my fancy. If my reason   555
Will thereto be obedient, I have reason;
If not, my senses, better pleased with madness,
Do bid it welcome.
    Cam.   This is desperate, sir.
    Flo. So call it: but it does fulfill my vow;   560
I needs must think it honesty. Camillo,
Not for Bohemia, nor the pomp that may
Be thereat gleaned; for all the sun sees or
The close earth wombs, or the profound seas hides
In unknown fathoms, will I break my oath   565
To this my fair beloved. Therefore, I pray you,
As you have ever been my father's honored friend,
When he shall miss me—as, in faith, I mean not
To see him any more—cast your good counsels
Upon his passion. Let myself and fortune   570
Tug for the time to come. This you may know
And so deliver; I am put to sea
With her who here I cannot hold on shore;
And most opportune to our need I have
A vessel rides fast by, but not prepared   575
For this design. What course I mean to hold
Shall nothing benefit your knowledge, nor
Concern me the reporting.
    Cam.   O my lord!

588. **Purchase:** gain; achieve.

592. **fraught:** burdened; **curious:** intricate; complicated.

600. **as thought on:** in accordance with his estimate of their worth.

604. **embrace:** accept; **direction:** suggestion.

605. **ponderous and settled:** determined after weighty consideration. Camillo is being tactful but ironic in so describing Florizel's sketchy plan.

607. **receiving:** reception.

I would your spirit were easier for advice,   580
Or stronger for your need.
    Flo.   Hark, Perdita.
                               [Drawing her aside.]
[To Camillo] I'll hear you by and by.
    Cam.   He's irremoveable,
Resolved for flight. Now were I happy if   585
His going I could frame to serve my turn,
Save him from danger, do him love and honor,
Purchase the sight again of dear Sicilia
And that unhappy King, my master, whom
I so much thirst to see.   590
    Flo.   Now, good Camillo,
I am so fraught with curious business that
I leave out ceremony.
    Cam.   Sir, I think
You have heard of my poor services i' the love   595
That I have borne your father?
    Flo.   Very nobly
Have you deserved: it is my father's music
To speak your deeds, not little of his care
To have them recompensed as thought on.   600
    Cam.   Well, my lord,
If you may please to think I love the King,
And through him what's nearest to him, which is
Your gracious self, embrace but my direction:
If your more ponderous and settled project   605
May suffer alteration, on mine honor
I'll point you where you shall have such receiving
As shall become your Highness; where you may
Enjoy your mistress, from the whom, I see,

611. **forfend:** forbid; **ruin:** destruction.

613. **discontenting:** discontented; **qualify:** moderate; temper.

622-23. **as the unthought-on accident is guilty/ To what we wildly do:** as the unexpected event (discovery of himself and Perdita by his father) is responsible for the hasty action they must take.

631. **habited:** clothed.

633. **free:** generous.

636-37. **divides him/ 'Twixt his unkindness and his kindness:** speaks alternately of his past cruelty to Florizel's father and his present kindness to Florizel himself.

There's no disjunction to be made but by—   610
As Heavens forfend!—your ruin. Marry her,
And, with my best endeavors in your absence,
Your discontenting father strive to qualify
And bring him up to liking.
    Flo.   How, Camillo,   615
May this, almost a miracle, be done?
That I may call thee something more than man
And after that trust to thee.
    Cam.   Have you thought on
A place whereto you'll go?   620
    Flo.   Not any yet;
But as the unthought-on accident is guilty
To what we wildly do, so we profess
Ourselves to be the slaves of chance and flies
Of every wind that blows.   625
    Cam.   Then list to me.
This follows, if you will not change your purpose
But undergo this flight, make for Sicilia
And there present yourself and your fair princess—
For so I see she must be—'fore Leontes.   630
She shall be habited as it becomes
The partner of your bed. Methinks I see
Leontes opening his free arms and weeping
His welcomes forth; asks thee there, son, forgiveness,
As 'twere i' the father's person; kisses the hands   635
Of your fresh princess; o'er and o'er divides him
'Twixt his unkindness and his kindness; the one
He chides to hell and bids the other grow
Faster than thought or time.
    Flo.   Worthy Camillo,   640

641. **color:** pretext.

650. **have your father's bosom there:** are completely in your father's confidence.

653. **sap:** vital fluid; therefore, probability of success.

659. **Nothing so certain:** by no means as secure.

667. **take in:** conquer.

What color for my visitation shall I
Hold up before him?
 Cam.   Sent by the King your father
To greet him and to give him comforts. Sir,
The manner of your bearing toward him, with   645
What you as from your father shall deliver,
Things known betwixt us three, I'll write you down:
The which shall point you forth at every sitting
What you must say; that he shall not perceive
But that you have your father's bosom there   650
And speak his very heart.
 Flo.   I am bound to you.
There is some sap in this.
 Cam.   A course more promising
Than a wild dedication of yourselves   655
To unpathed waters, undreamed shores, most certain
To miseries enough: no hope to help you,
But as you shake off one to take another;
Nothing so certain as your anchors, who
Do their best office if they can but stay you   660
Where you'll be loath to be. Besides, you know
Prosperity's the very bond of love,
Whose fresh complexion and whose heart together
Affliction alters.
 Per. One of these is true.   665
I think affliction may subdue the cheek,
But not take in the mind.
 Cam.   Yea, say you so?
There shall not at your father's house these seven
  years   670
Be born another such.

673-74. **as forward of her breeding as/ She is i' the rear' our birth:** as superior to her origins as she is beneath me in birth.

683. **medicine:** doctor.

695. **pomander:** round case in which scented herbs or perfume might be carried; **table book:** notebook.

Flo.   My good Camillo,
She is as forward of her breeding as
She is i' the rear' our birth.
　　Cam.   I cannot say 'tis pity   675
She lacks instructions, for she seems a mistress
To most that teach.
　　Per.   Your pardon, sir: for this
I'll blush you thanks.
　　Flo.   My prettiest Perdita!   680
But, oh, the thorns we stand upon! Camillo,
Preserver of my father, now of me,
The medicine of our house, how shall we do?
We are not furnished like Bohemia's son,
Nor shall appear in Sicilia.   685
　　Cam.   My lord,
Fear none of this. I think you know my fortunes
Do all lie there. It shall be so my care
To have you royally appointed as if
The scene you play were mine. For instance, sir,   690
That you may know you shall not want, one word.

　　　　　　　　　　　　　[They talk aside.]

Enter Autolycus.

　　Aut. Ha, ha! what a fool Honesty is! and Trust, his
sworn brother, a very simple gentleman! I have sold
all my trumpery: not a counterfeit stone, not a ribbon,
glass, pomander, brooch, table book, ballad, knife,   695
tape, glove, shoe tie, bracelet, horn ring, to keep my
pack from fasting. They throng who should buy first,
as if my trinkets had been hallowed and brought a

700. **best in picture:** most visible (and, perhaps, fullest.

707-8. **geld a codpiece of a purse:** cut a purse from the front placket of a man's breeches. Codpieces were sometimes large enough to be used as pockets.

713. **whoobub:** hubbub.

714. **choughs:** jackdaws.

benediction to the buyer; by which means I saw
whose purse was best in picture; and what I saw to 700
my good use I remembered. My clown, who wants
but something to be a reasonable man, grew so in
love with the wenches' song that he would not
stir his pettitoes till he had both tune and words;
which so drew the rest of the herd to me that all their 705
other senses stuck in ears. You might have pinched a
placket, it was senseless; 'twas nothing to geld a codpiece of a purse; I would have filed keys off that hung
in chains. No hearing, no feeling, but my sir's song,
and admiring the nothing of it. So that in this time of 710
lethargy I picked and cut most of their festival
purses; and had not the old man come in with a
whoobub against his daughter and the King's son and
scared my choughs from the chaff, I had not left a
purse alive in the whole army.   715

[*Camillo, Florizel, and Perdita come forward.*]

  Cam. Nay, but my letters, by this means being
      there
So soon as you arrive, shall clear that doubt.
  Flo. And those that you'll procure from King Leon-
      tes—   720
  Cam. Shall satisfy your father.
  Per.   Happy be you!
All that you speak shows fair.
  Cam.   Who have we here?
                          [*Seeing Autolycus.*]

738. **boot:** reward; profit.
741. **dispatch:** hurry.
746. **earnest:** partial payment.
753. **disliken:** disguise.
754. **seeming:** appearance.

We'll make an instrument of this; omit   725
Nothing may give us aid.

    Aut. [*Aside*] If they have overheard me now, why,
hanging.

    Cam. How now, good fellow! Why shakest thou so?
Fear not, man: here's no harm intended to thee.   730

    Aut. I am a poor fellow, sir.

    Cam. Why, be so still. Here's nobody will steal
that from thee. Yet for the outside of thy poverty we
must make an exchange: therefore discase thee instantly—thou must think there's a necessity in't—and 735
change garments with this gentleman. Though the
pennyworth on his side be the worst, yet hold thee,
there's some boot.

    Aut. I am a poor fellow, sir. [*Aside*] I know ye well
enough.   740

    Cam. Nay, prithee, dispatch. The gentleman is half
flayed already.

    Aut. Are you in earnest, sir? [*Aside*] I smell the
trick on't.

    Flo. Dispatch, I prithee.   745

    Aut. Indeed, I have had earnest; but I cannot with
conscience take it.

    Cam. Unbuckle, unbuckle.

        [*Florizel and Autolycus exchange garments.*]
Fortunate mistress—let my prophecy
Come home to ye!—you must retire yourself   750
Into some covert. Take your sweetheart's hat
And pluck it o'er your brows, muffle your face,
Dismantle you, and, as you can, disliken
The truth of your own seeming; that you may—

755. **eyes over:** espial (by the King's agents).
782. **unjust:** dishonest.

For I do fear eyes over—to shipboard   755
Get undescried.
   Per.   I see the play so lies
That I must bear a part.
   Cam.   No remedy.
Have you done there?   760
   Flo.   Should I now meet my father,
He would not call me son.
   Cam.   Nay, you shall have no hat.
               [*Giving it to Perdita.*]
Come, lady, come. Farewell, my friend.
   Aut.   Adieu, sir.   765
   Flo. O Perdita, what have we twain forgot!
Pray you, a word.
   Cam. [*Aside*]..What I do next shall be to tell the
     King
Of this escape and whither they are bound;   770
Wherein my hope is I shall so prevail
To force him after: in whose company
I shall review Sicilia, for whose sight
I have a woman's longing.
   Flo.   Fortune speed us!   775
Thus we set on, Camillo, to the seaside.
   Cam. The swifter speed the better.
       [*Exeunt Florizel, Perdita, and Camillo.*]
   Aut. I understand the business, I hear it. To have an
open ear, a quick eye, and a nimble hand is necessary
for a cutpurse; a good nose is requisite also, to smell 780
out work for the other senses. I see this is the time
that the unjust man doth thrive. What an exchange
had this been without boot! What a boot is here with

784. **connive at:** wink at; indulge.
787. **clog:** impediment (Perdita).
795. **changeling:** foundling.
799. **Go to:** very well.

this exchange! Sure the gods do this year connive at
us, and we may do anything extempore. The Prince   785
himself is about a piece of iniquity, stealing away
from his father with his clog at his heels. If I thought
it were a piece of honesty to acquaint the King withal,
I would not do't. I hold it the more knavery to conceal
it; and therein am I constant to my profession.   790

Enter Clown and Shepherd.

Aside, aside! Here is more matter for a hot brain.
Every lane's end, every shop, church, session, hanging, yields a careful man work.

 Clo. See, see; what a man you are now! There is no
other way but to tell the King she's a changeling and   795
none of your flesh and blood.

 Shep. Nay, but hear me.

 Clo. Nay, but hear me.

 Shep. Go to, then.

 Clo. She being none of your flesh and blood, your   800
flesh and blood has not offended the King; and so
your flesh and blood is not to be punished by him.
Show those things you found about her, those secret
things, all but what she has with her. This being
done, let the law go whistle. I warrant you.   805

 Shep. I will tell the King all, every word, yea, and
his son's pranks too; who, I may say, is no honest man,
neither to his father nor to me, to go about to make
me the King's brother-in-law.

 Clo. Indeed, brother-in-law was the farthest off you   810

815. **fardel:** bundle.

821. **excrement:** outgrowth of hair.

823. **and:** if; **like:** please.

830-33. **they often give us soldiers the lie; but we pay them for it with stamped coin, not stabbing steel; therefore they do not give us the lie:** they often cheat us soldiers, but we pay them for it with current money, not by stabbing them; therefore they do not give us the lie (but sell it to us). There is a pun on another meaning of "give the lie," to accuse of lying; the soldier's response to such an accusation would be a stab.

835. **taken yourself with the manner:** caught yourself in the act (and corrected the statement about the tradesmen giving soldiers the lie). In legal terminology a **manner,** or "mainour," was a piece of stolen property.

could have been to him and then your blood had been
the dearer by I know how much an ounce.

Aut. [*Aside*] Very wisely, puppies!

Shep. Well, let us to the King. There is that in this
fardel will make him scratch his beard.   815

Aut. [*Aside*] I know not what impediment this
complaint may be to the flight of my master.

Clo. Pray heartily he be at 'palace.

Aut. [*Aside*] Though I am not naturally honest, I
am so sometimes by chance. Let me pocket up my   820
peddler's excrement.   [*Takes off his false beard.*]
How now, rustics; whither are you bound?

Shep. To the palace, and it like your Worship.

Aut. Your affairs there, with whom, the condition
of that fardel, the place of your dwelling, your names,   825
your ages, of what having, breeding, and anything
that is fitting to be known, discover.

Clo. We are but plain fellows, sir.

Aut. A lie: you are rough and hairy. Let me have
no lying: it becomes none but tradesmen, and they   830
often give us soldiers the lie; but we pay them for it
with stamped coin, not stabbing steel; therefore they
do not give us the lie.

Clo. Your Worship had like to have given us one, if
you had not taken yourself with the manner.   835

Shep. Are you a courtier, and't like you, sir?

Aut. Whether it like me or no, I am a courtier.
Seest thou not the air of the court in these enfoldings?
Hath not my gait in it the measure of the court? Re-
ceives not thy nose court odor from me? Reflect I not   840

842. **insinuate:** coax; **toaze:** tease.

843. **cap-a-pe:** from head to foot.

845. **open:** reveal.

849. **Advocate's the court word for a pheasant:** thinking of a court of law, the Clown suggests that a pheasant would be a suitable bribe for the judge.

858-59. **fantastical:** whimsical; eccentric.

on thy baseness court contempt? Thinkst thou, for
that I insinuate, or toaze from thee thy business, I am
therefore no courtier? I am courtier cap-a-pe; and one
that will either push on or pluck back thy business
there. Whereupon I command thee to open thy affair. 845

Shep. My business, sir, is to the King.

Aut. What advocate hast thou to him?

Shep. I know not, and't like you.

Clo. Advocate's the court word for a pheasant: say
you have none.   850

Shep. None, sir; I have no pheasant, cock nor hen.

Aut. How blessed are we that are not simple men!
Yet nature might have made me as these are,
Therefore I will not disdain.

Clo. This cannot be but a great courtier.   855

Shep. His garments are rich, but he wears them not
handsomely.

Clo. He seems to be the more noble in being fantastical. A great man, I'll warrant: I know by the picking on's teeth.   860

Aut. The fardel there? What's i' the fardel? Wherefore that box?

Shep. Sir, there lies such secrets in this fardel and
box, which none must know but the King; and which
he shall know within this hour, if I may come to the 865
speech of him.

Aut. Age, thou hast lost thy labor.

Shep. Why, sir?

Aut. The King is not at the palace; he is gone
aboard a new ship to purge melancholy and air him- 870

875. **in handfast:** arrested.

880-81. **germane:** related.

892. **a dram:** a bit more.

895. **prognostication:** i.e., an almanac.

900. **capital:** worthy of death.

901. **what you have to:** what business you have with.

Shearing sheep. From T[homas] F[ella], "A Book of Divers Devices" (1585-1622; Folger MS V.a. 311).

self. For, if thou beest capable of things serious, thou
must know the King is full of grief.

Shep. So 'tis said, sir; about his son, that should
have married a shepherd's daughter.

Aut. If that shepherd be not in handfast, let him 875
fly! The curses he shall have, the tortures he shall feel,
will break the back of man, the heart of monster.

Clo. Think you so, sir?

Aut. Not he alone shall suffer what wit can make
heavy and vengeance bitter; but those that are ger- 880
mane to him, though removed fifty times, shall all
come under the hangman: which, though it be great
pity, yet it is necessary. An old sheep-whistling rogue,
a ram tender, to offer to have his daughter come into
grace! Some say he shall be stoned; but that death is 885
too soft for him, say I. Draw our throne into a sheep-
cote! All deaths are too few, the sharpest too easy.

Clo. Has the old man e'er a son, sir, do you hear,
and't like you, sir?

Aut. He has a son, who shall be flayed alive; then, 890
'nointed over with honey, set on the head of a wasp's
nest; then stand till he be three quarters and a dram
dead; then recovered again with aqua vitae or some
other hot infusion; then, raw as he is, and in the hot-
test day prognostication proclaims, shall he be set 895
against a brick wall, the sun looking with a south-
ward eye upon him, where he is to behold him with
flies blown to death. But what talk we of these traitor-
ly rascals, whose miseries are to be smiled at, their
offenses being so capital? Tell me, for you seem to be 900
honest plain men, what you have to the King. Being

902. **something gently considered:** somewhat civilly rewarded (a subtle hint for a bribe).

906. **Close:** settle.

920. **case:** skin.

something gently considered, I'll bring you where he
is aboard, tender your persons to his presence, whisper him in your behalfs; and if it be in man besides
the King to effect your suits, here is man shall do it. 905

Clo. He seems to be of great authority. Close with
him, give him gold; and though authority be a stub-
born bear, yet he is oft led by the nose with gold.
Show the inside of your purse to the outside of his
hand, and no more ado. Remember "stoned," and 910
"flayed alive."

Shep. And't please you, sir, to undertake the business for us, here is that gold I have. I'll make it as
much more and leave this young man in pawn till I
bring it you. 915

Aut. After I have done what I promised?

Shep. Ay, sir.

Aut. Well, give me the moiety. Are you a party in
this business?

Clo. In some sort, sir: but though my case be a piti- 920
ful one, I hope I shall not be flayed out of it.

Aut. Oh, that's the case of the shepherd's son.
Hang him, he'll be made an example.

Clo. Comfort, good comfort! We must to the King
and show our strange sights. He must know 'tis none 925
of your daughter nor my sister; we are gone else. Sir,
I will give you as much as this old man does when the
business is performed, and remain, as he says, your
pawn till it be brought you.

Aut. I will trust you. Walk toward the seaside; go 930
on the right hand: I will but look upon the hedge and
follow you.

943. shore them: put them ashore.

Clo. [*Aside to Shepherd*] We are blest in this man, as I may say, even blest.

Shep. Let's before as he bids us. He was provided 935
to do us good.   [*Exeunt Shepherd and Clown.*]

Aut. If I had a mind to be honest, I see Fortune
would not suffer me: she drops booties in my mouth.
I am courted now with a double occasion, gold and a
means to do the Prince my master good; which who 940
knows how that may turn back to my advancement? I
will bring these two moles, these blind ones, aboard
him. If he think it fit to shore them again and that the
complaint they have to the King concerns him nothing, let him call me rogue for being so far officious; 945
for I am proof against that title and what shame else
belongs to't. To him will I present them: there may
be matter in it.

Exit.

THE
WINTER'S
TALE

ACT V

V.i. Leontes, grieving over the deaths of his wife and son, promises Paulina not to marry without her consent. She hints that she can choose a queen for him that will resemble his first wife, Hermione. Florizel and Perdita arrive and are welcomed by Leontes. Polixenes has followed, and Leontes soon learns that the lovers are fugitives. Leontes promises Florizel that he will help him to marry Perdita if his conduct has been honorable.

||||||||||||||||||||||||||||||||||||||||||

10. **blemishes in them:** i.e., faults in falsely accusing them.

ACT V

Scene I. [Sicilia. A room in Leontes' palace.]

Enter Leontes, Cleomenes, Dion, Paulina, and Servants.

Cleo. Sir, you have done enough, and have per-
    formed
A saint-like sorrow. No fault could you make
Which you have not redeemed; indeed, paid down
More penitence than done trespass. At the last,   5
Do as the Heavens have done, forget your evil;
With them, forgive yourself.

Leon.   Whilst I remember
Her and her virtues, I cannot forget
My blemishes in them, and so still think of   10
The wrong I did myself: which was so much
That heirless it hath made my kingdom and
Destroyed the sweet'st companion that e'er man
Bred his hopes out of.

Paul.   True, too true, my lord.   15
If, one by one, you wedded all the world,
Or from the all that are took something good
To make a perfect woman, she you killed
Would be unparalleled.

23. **good now:** if you will be so good now.

36. **Incertain lookers-on:** bystanders who do not know how to deal with the situation; the helpless subjects of the land; **were:** would be.

38. **for royalty's repair:** to restore the state of royalty (by providing an heir).

43. **Respecting:** in comparison with.

49. **monstrous:** miraculous.

   Leon.   I think so. Killed!   20
She I killed! I did so; but thou strikest me
Sorely, to say I did: it is as bitter
Upon thy tongue as in my thought. Now, good now,
Say so but seldom.
   Cleo.   Not at all, good lady.   25
You might have spoken a thousand things that would
Have done the time more benefit and graced
Your kindness better.
   Paul.   You are one of those
Would have him wed again.   30
   Dion.   If you would not so,
You pity not the state nor the remembrance
Of his most sovereign name; consider little
What dangers, by His Highness' fail of issue,
May drop upon his kingdom and devour   35
Incertain lookers-on. What were more holy
Than to rejoice the former Queen is well?
What holier than, for royalty's repair,
For present comfort and for future good,
To bless the bed of majesty again   40
With a sweet fellow to't?
   Paul.   There is none worthy,
Respecting her that's gone. Besides, the gods
Will have fulfilled their secret purposes;
For has not the divine Apollo said,   45
Is't not the tenor of his oracle,
That King Leontes shall not have an heir
Till his lost child be found? Which, that it shall,
Is all as monstrous to our human reason
As my Antigonus to break his grave   50

62. **squared me:** fitted myself.

63. **looked upon my queen's full eyes:** i.e., instead of imagining them closed in death.

71. **Where we offenders now:** where we are now offenders.

And come again to me; who, on my life,
Did perish with the infant. 'Tis your counsel
My lord should to the Heavens be contrary,
Oppose against their wills. [*To Leontes*] Care not for
    issue: 55
The crown will find an heir. Great Alexander
Left his to the worthiest; so his successor
Was like to be the best.
    Leon.   Good Paulina,
Who hast the memory of Hermione,   60
I know, in honor, oh, that ever I
Had squared me to thy counsel! Then, even now,
I might have looked upon my queen's full eyes;
Have taken treasure from her lips—
    Paul.   And left them   65
More rich for what they yielded.
    Leon.   Thou speakst truth.
No more such wives; therefore, no wife. One worse,
And better used, would make her sainted spirit
Again possess her corpse, and on this stage,   70
Where we offenders now, appear soul-vexed,
And begin, "Why to me?"
    Paul.   Had she such power,
She had just cause.
    Leon.   She had; and would incense me   75
To murder her I married.
    Paul.   I should so.
Were I the ghost that walked, I'ld bid you mark
Her eye and tell me for what dull part in't
You chose her; then I'ld shriek, that even your ears   80

82. **mine:** i.e., her eyes.

93. **Affront:** come before.

100. **walked your first queen's ghost:** if your first queen's ghost walked.

107. **gives out himself:** claims to be.

Should rift to hear me; and the words that followed
Should be "Remember mine."

    Leon.   Stars, stars,
And all eyes else dead coals! Fear thou no wife;
I'll have no wife, Paulina.   85

    Paul.   Will you swear
Never to marry but by my free leave?

    Leon. Never, Paulina; so be blest my spirit!

    Paul. Then, good my lords, bear witness to his oath.

    Cleo. You tempt him overmuch.   90

    Paul.   Unless another,
As like Hermione as is her picture,
Affront his eye.

    Cleo.   Good madam—

    Paul.   I have done.   95
Yet, if my lord will marry—if you will, sir,
No remedy, but you will—give me the office
To choose you a queen. She shall not be so young
As was your former; but she shall be such
As, walked your first queen's ghost, it should take joy 100
To see her in your arms.

    Leon.   My true Paulina,
We shall not marry till you biddst us.

    Paul.   That
Shall be when your first queen's again in breath; 105
Never till then.

Enter a Servant.

    Ser. One that gives out himself Prince Florizel,
Son of Polixenes, with his princess, she

113. **out of circumstance:** unceremonious.

114. **framed:** planned.

126. **that theme:** the dead Hermione.

128. **'Tis shrewdly ebbed:** i.e., the flow of your verse in honor of Hermione has sharply reversed itself.

133. **tongue:** praise.

135. **professors else:** professors of other faiths.

The fairest I have yet beheld, desires access
To your high presence.   110
   Leon.   What with him? He comes not
Like to his father's greatness. His approach,
So out of circumstance and sudden, tells us
'Tis not a visitation framed, but forced
By need and accident. What train?   115
   Ser.   But few,
And those but mean.
   Leon.   His princess, say you, with him?
   Ser. Ay, the most peerless piece of earth, I think,
That e'er the sun shone bright on.   120
   Paul.   O Hermione,
As every present time doth boast itself
Above a better gone, so must thy grave
Give way to what's seen now! Sir, you yourself
Have said and writ so, but your writing now   125
Is colder than that theme, "She had not been,
Nor was not to be equaled"—thus your verse
Flowed with her beauty once. 'Tis shrewdly ebbed,
To say you have seen a better.
   Ser.   Pardon, madam.   130
The one I have almost forgot—your pardon—
The other, when she has obtained your eye,
Will have your tongue too. This is a creature,
Would she begin a sect, might quench the zeal
Of all professors else; make proselytes   135
Of who she but bid follow.
   Paul.   How! not women?
   Ser. Women will love her that she is a woman

139. **worth**: worthy.

More worth than any man; men, that she is
The rarest of all women.   140
   Leon.   Go, Cleomenes;
Yourself, assisted with your honored friends,
Bring them to our embracement.
               [*Exeunt Cleomenes and others.*]
                    Still, 'tis strange
He thus should steal upon us.   145
   Paul.   Had our prince,
Jewel of children, seen this hour, he had paired
Well with this lord. There was not full a month
Between their births.
   Leon. Prithee, no more; cease! Thou knowst   150
He dies to me again when talked of. Sure,
When I shall see this gentleman, thy speeches
Will bring me to consider that which may
Unfurnish me of reason. They are come.

Enter Florizel, Perdita, Cleomenes, and others.

Your mother was most true to wedlock, Prince;   155
For she did print your royal father off,
Conceiving you. Were I but twenty-one,
Your father's image is so hit in you,
His very air, that I should call you brother,
As I did him, and speak of something wildly   160
By us performed before. Most dearly welcome!
And your fair princess—goddess!—Oh, alas!
I lost a couple that twixt heaven and earth
Might thus have stood begetting wonder, as
You, gracious couple, do: and then I lost,   165

167. **brave:** gallant; splendid.

172. **at friend:** as a friend, or, in a friendly way.

174. **waits upon worn times:** accompanies old age.

174-75. **something seized/ His wished ability:** somewhat mastered the strength he would like to have.

175. **had:** would have.

177. **Measured:** traveled.

182. **offices:** offerings of friendly greetings.

183. **interpreters:** reminders.

All mine own folly, the society,
Amity too, of your brave father, whom,
Though bearing misery, I desire my life
Once more to look on him.
   Flo.   By his command   170
Have I here touched Sicilia, and from him
Give you all greetings that a king, at friend,
Can send his brother: and, but infirmity,
Which waits upon worn times, hath something seized
His wished ability, he had himself   175
The lands and waters 'twixt your throne and his
Measured to look upon you; whom he loves,
He bade me say so, more than all the scepters
And those that bear them living.
   Leon.   O my brother,   180
Good gentleman! the wrongs I have done thee stir
Afresh within me; and these thy offices,
So rarely kind, are as interpreters
Of my behindhand slackness! Welcome hither,
As is the spring to the earth. And hath he too   185
Exposed this paragon to the fearful usage,
At least ungentle, of the dreadful Neptune,
To greet a man not worth her pains, much less
The adventure of her person?
   Flo.   Good my lord,   190
She came from Libya.
   Leon.   Where the warlike Smalus,
That noble honored lord, is feared and loved?
   Flo. Most royal sir, from thence; from him whose
      daughter   195
His tears proclaimed his, parting with her. Thence,

207. **climate:** abide; visit.
208. **graceful:** gracious; virtuous.
217. **bear no credit:** be disbelieved.
219. **Bohemia:** the King of Bohemia.
220. **attach:** arrest.

A prosperous south wind friendly, we have crossed,
To execute the charge my father gave me,
For visiting your Highness. My best train
I have from your Sicilian shores dismissed;   200
Who for Bohemia bend, to signify
Not only my success in Libya, sir,
But my arrival, and my wife's, in safety
Here where we are.
   Leon.   The blessed gods   205
Purge all infection from our air whilst you
Do climate here! You have a holy father,
A graceful gentleman; against whose person,
So sacred as it is, I have done sin:
For which the Heavens, taking angry note,   210
Have left me issueless; and your father's blest,
As he from Heaven merits it, with you
Worthy his goodness. What might I have been,
Might I a son and daughter now have looked on,
Such goodly things as you!   215

Enter a Lord.

   Lord.   Most noble sir,
That which I shall report will bear no credit,
Were not the proof so nigh. Please you, great sir,
Bohemia greets you from himself by me;
Desires you to attach his son, who has—   220
His dignity and duty both cast off—
Fled from his father, from his hopes, and with
A shepherd's daughter.
   Leon.   Where's Bohemia? Speak.

226. **becomes:** is appropriate to.

227. **My marvel:** the wonder I feel.

240. **in question:** under questioning.

249. **like:** likely.

251. **The odds for high and low's alike:** the chances of highborn and lowborn being able to marry are as remote as is the possibility of the stars reaching down to kiss the valleys.

255. **When once she is my wife:** the term "daughter" was also used for daughter-in-law.

Lord. Here in your city: I now come from him.   225
I speak amazedly; and it becomes
My marvel and my message. To your court
Whiles he was hast'ning, in the chase, it seems,
Of this fair couple, meets he on the way
The father of this seeming lady and   230
Her brother, having both their country quitted
With this young prince.

Flo.   Camillo has betrayed me;
Whose honor and whose honesty till now
Endured all weathers.   235

Lord.   Lay't so to his charge.
He's with the King your father.

Leon.   Who? Camillo?

Lord. Camillo, sir; I spake with him; who now
Has these poor men in question. Never saw I   240
Wretches so quake: they kneel, they kiss the earth,
Forswear themselves as often as they speak.
Bohemia stops his ears and threatens them
With divers deaths in death.

Per.   O my poor father!   245
The Heaven sets spies upon us, will not have
Our contract celebrated.

Leon.   You are married?

Flo. We are not, sir, nor are we like to be.
The stars, I see, will kiss the valleys first: 250
The odds for high and low's alike.

Leon.   My lord,
Is this the daughter of a king?

Flo.   She is,
When once she is my wife.   255

259. **broken from his liking:** displeased him.

263. **look up:** be cheerful.

264. **visible:** visibly.

267. **since:** when.

267-68. **owed no more time/ Than I do now:** were as young as I am.

268. **such affections:** youthful passions.

281. **to:** i.e., go to.

282. **Your honor not o'erthrown by your desires:** i.e., provided that your desires have been honorably restrained, or are being sought by honorable means.

285. **mark what way I make:** observe how I succeed.

Leon. That "once," I see by your good father's
     speed,
Will come on very slowly. I am sorry,
Most sorry, you have broken from his liking,
Where you were tied in duty, and as sorry   260
Your choice is not so rich in worth as beauty,
That you might well enjoy her.
     Flo.   Dear, look up.
Though Fortune, visible an enemy,
Should chase us with my father, pow'r no jot   265
Hath she to change our loves. Beseech you, sir,
Remember since you owed no more to time
Than I do now. With thought of such affections,
Step forth mine advocate: at your request
My father will grant precious things as trifles.   270
     Leon. Would he do so, I'ld beg your precious mis-
     tress,
Which he counts but a trifle.
     Paul.   Sir, my Liege,
Your eye hath too much youth in't. Not a month   275
'Fore your queen died, she was more worth such gazes
Than what you look on now.
     Leon.   I thought of her,
Even in these looks I made. [*To Florizel*] But your
     petition   280
Is yet unanswered. I will to your father.
Your honor not o'erthrown by your desires,
I am friend to them and you. Upon which errand
I now go toward him: therefore follow me
And mark what way I make. Come, good my lord.   285
                              Exeunt.

V.ii. A conversation between Autolycus and courtiers reveals that the shepherds have disclosed the secret of Perdita's birth. Leontes has recognized the mantle in which she was wrapped. Perdita's resemblance to her dead mother confirms the evidence that she is the King's lost daughter. Leontes and Polixenes are joyfully reconciled. Perdita has heard of a remarkably lifelike statue of Hermione, made for Paulina by a famous Italian master, and the party has gone to view it.

‖‖‖‖‖‖‖‖‖‖‖‖‖‖‖‖‖‖‖‖‖‖‖‖‖

12. **very:** absolute; **notes of admiration:** signs of wonder.

13. **cases:** rims; lids.

15. **as:** as if.

18. **seeing:** what he could see.

19. **importance:** import; meaning.

19-20. **in the extremity of the one, it must needs be:** whichever emotion was the cause was felt to the utmost degree.

21. **happily:** perhaps.

Scene II. [Before Leontes' palace.]

Enter Autolycus and a Gentleman.

Aut. Beseech you, sir, were you present at this
relation?

1. Gent. I was by at the opening of the fardel,
heard the old shepherd deliver the manner how he
found it: whereupon, after a little amazedness, we   5
were all commanded out of the chamber; only this
methought I heard the shepherd say, he found the
child.

Aut. I would most gladly know the issue of it.

1. Gent. I make a broken delivery of the business;   10
but the changes I perceived in the King and Camillo
were very notes of admiration. They seemed almost,
with staring on one another, to tear the cases of their
eyes. There was speech in their dumbness, language
in their very gesture. They looked as they had heard   15
of a world ransomed, or one destroyed. A notable passion of wonder appeared in them; but the wisest be-
holder, that knew no more but seeing, could not say if
the importance were joy or sorrow; but in the extremity of the one, it must needs be.   20

Enter another Gentleman.

Here comes a gentleman that happily knows more.
The news, Rogero?

23. **bonfires:** i.e., such news as calls for celebration.

32-3. **pregnant by circumstance:** enlarged by circumstantial detail.

34. **unity:** accord.

37. **character:** handwriting.

38. **affection of nobleness:** characteristic nobility.

49-50. **countenance of such distraction:** such agitated facial expressions.

2. Gent. Nothing but bonfires. The oracle is fulfilled: the King's daughter is found. Such a deal of
wonder is broken out within this hour that ballad   25
makers cannot be able to express it.

Enter a third Gentleman.

Here comes the Lady Paulina's steward: he can deliver you more. How goes it now, sir? This news
which is called true is so like an old tale that the
verity of it is in strong suspicion. Has the King found   30
his heir?

3. Gent. Most true, if ever truth were pregnant by
circumstance. That which you hear you'll swear you
see, there is such unity in the proofs. The mantle of
Queen Hermione's, her jewel about the neck of it, the   35
letters of Antigonus found with it, which they know
to be his character, the majesty of the creature in resemblance of the mother, the affection of nobleness
which nature shows above her breeding, and many
other evidences proclaim her with all certainty to be   40
the King's daughter. Did you see the meeting of the
two Kings?

2. Gent. No.

3. Gent. Then have you lost a sight which was to be
seen, cannot be spoken of. There might you have be-   45
held one joy crown another, so and in such manner
that it seemed sorrow wept to take leave of them, for
their joy waded in tears. There was casting up of eyes,
holding up of hands, with countenance of such distraction that they were to be known by garment, not   50

51. **favor:** characteristic appearance.

56. **clipping:** embracing.

57. **weather-bitten:** weather-beaten; **conduit:** fountain. The tearful shepherd is compared to a waterspout in human form.

60. **do:** achieve.

63-5. **will have matter to rehearse, though credit be asleep and not an ear open:** enumerates a great deal of material impossible to be believed.

66-7. **innocence:** simple-mindedness.

by favor. Our king, being ready to leap out of himself
for joy of his found daughter, as if that joy were now
become a loss, cries, "Oh, thy mother, thy mother!"
then asks Bohemia forgiveness; then embraces his
son-in-law; then again worries he his daughter with 55
clipping her; now he thanks the old shepherd, which
stands by like a weather-bitten conduit of many kings'
reigns. I never heard of such another encounter,
which lames report to follow it and undoes description to do it. 60

2. Gent. What, pray you, became of Antigonus, that
carried hence the child?

3. Gent. Like an old tale still, which will have
matter to rehearse, though credit be asleep and not
an ear open. He was torn to pieces with a bear. This 65
avouches the shepherd's son, who has not only his innocence, which seems much, to justify him, but a
handkerchief and rings of his that Paulina knows.

1. Gent. What became of his bark and his followers? 70

3. Gent. Wracked the same instant of their master's
death and in the view of the shepherd: so that all the
instruments which aided to expose the child were
even then lost when it was found. But, oh, the noble
combat that 'twixt joy and sorrow was fought in 75
Paulina! She had one eye declined for the loss of her
husband, another elevated that the oracle was fulfilled. She lifted the Princess from the earth and so
locks her in embracing as if she would pin her to her
heart, that she might no more be in danger of losing. 80

84. **the water:** tears.

87-8. **attentiveness:** rapt attention.

98. **Julio Romano:** a well-known sixteenth-century Italian artist.

100. **custom:** trade; business.

101. **ape:** imitator.

104. **sup:** i.e., feed their emotion.

107-8. **removed:** secluded.

109. **piece:** add to.

111. **grace:** miracle.

1. Gent. The dignity of this act was worth the audience of kings and princes; for by such was it acted.

3. Gent. One of the prettiest touches of all, and that which angled for mine eyes, caught the water though not the fish, was when, at the relation of the Queen's 85 death, with the manner how she came to't bravely confessed and lamented by the King, how attentiveness wounded his daughter; till, from one sign of dolor to another, she did, with an "Alas!" I would fain say, bleed tears, for I am sure my heart wept blood. 90 Who was most marble there changed color; some swooned, all sorrowed. If all the world could have seen't, the woe had been universal.

1. Gent. Are they returned to the court?

3. Gent. No; the Princess hearing of her mother's 95 statue, which is in the keeping of Paulina—a piece many years in doing and now newly performed by that rare Italian master, Julio Romano, who, had he himself eternity and could put breath into his work, would beguile Nature of her custom, so perfectly he 100 is her ape: he so near to Hermione hath done Hermione that they say one would speak to her and stand in hope of answer—thither with all greediness of affection are they gone, and there they intend to sup.

2. Gent. I thought she had some great matter there 105 in hand; for she hath privately twice or thrice a day, ever since the death of Hermione, visited that removed house. Shall we thither and with our company piece the rejoicing?

1. Gent. Who would be thence that has the benefit 110 of access? Every wink of an eye some new grace will

112-13. **unthrifty to our knowledge:** negligent of the chance to enlarge our own knowledge.

114. **dash:** taint.

115. **preferment:** promotion; advancement.

116. **the Prince:** i.e., the Prince's bark.

121. **undiscovered:** unexplored.

123. **relished:** been appreciated; i.e., his misdeeds would have spoiled its effect.

128. **past mo children:** past the age to have additional children.

be born. Our absence makes us unthrifty to our
knowledge. Let's along.   *Exeunt Gentlemen.*

Aut. Now, had I not the dash of my former life in
me, would preferment drop on my head. I brought 115
the old man and his son aboard the Prince; told him
I heard them talk of a fardel and I know not what:
but he at that time, overfond of the shepherd's daughter, so he then took her to be, who began to be much
seasick, and himself little better, extremity of weather 120
continuing, this mystery remained undiscovered. But
'tis all one to me; for had I been the finder-out of this
secret, it would not have relished among my other dis-
credits.

Enter Shepherd and Clown.

Here come those I have done good to against my will, 125
and already appearing in the blossoms of their fortune.

Shep. Come, boy. I am past mo children, but thy
sons and daughters will be all gentlemen born.

Clo. You are well met, sir. You denied to fight with 130
me this other day, because I was no gentleman born.
See you these clothes? Say you see them not and think
me still no gentleman born. You were best say these
robes are not gentlemen born. Give me the lie, do,
and try whether I am not now a gentleman born. 135

Aut. I know you are now, sir, a gentleman born.

Clo. Ay, and have been so any time these four
hours.

Shep. And so have I, boy.

148-49. **preposterous:** i.e., prosperous.
153. **gentle:** gracious; courteous.
156. **and it like:** if it please.
160. **boors:** peasants.
161. **franklins:** yeomen; small farmers.
165. **tall:** brave.

Clo. So you have: but I was a gentleman born be- 140
fore my father; for the King's son took me by the
hand and called me brother; and then the two kings
called my father brother; and then the Prince my
brother and the Princess my sister called my father
father; and so we wept, and there was the first gentle- 145
man-like tears that ever we shed.

Shep. We may live, son, to shed many more.

Clo. Ay, or else 'twere hard luck, being in so preposterous estate as we are.

Aut. I humbly beseech you, sir, to pardon me all 150
the faults I have committed to your Worship, and to
give me your good report to the Prince my master.

Shep. Prithee, son, do; for we must be gentle, now
we are gentlemen.

Clo. Thou wilt amend thy life? 155

Aut. Ay, and it like your good Worship.

Clo. Give me thy hand. I will swear to the Prince
thou art as honest a true fellow as any is in Bohemia.

Shep. You may say it, but not swear it.

Clo. Not swear it, now I am a gentleman? Let boors 160
and franklins say it; I'll swear it.

Shep. How if it be false, son?

Clo. If it be ne'er so false, a true gentleman may
swear it in the behalf of his friend: and I'll swear to
the Prince thou art a tall fellow of thy hands and that 165
thou wilt not be drunk; but I know thou art no tall
fellow of thy hands and that thou wilt be drunk: but
I'll swear it, and I would thou wouldst be a tall fellow
of thy hands.

Aut. I will prove so, sir, to my power. 170

V.iii. All are amazed at the resemblance of Paulina's statue to Hermione. When Leontes is determined to kiss the likeness of his wife, Paulina orders the statue to move, and Hermione descends from the pedestal. Amidst general joy, Leontes suggests that Camillo marry the faithful Paulina.

<hr style="width:30%; border-top: dotted;" />

5. **home:** in full.
6. **contracted:** betrothed.
13. **content:** pleasure.

Clo. Ay, by any means prove a tall fellow. If I do
not wonder how thou darest venture to be drunk, not
being a tall fellow, trust me not. Hark! the kings and
the princes, our kindred, are going to see the Queen's
picture. Come, follow us: we'll be thy good masters.   175
                                Exeunt.

Scene III. [A chapel in Paulina's house.]

Enter Leontes, Polixenes, Florizel, Perdita, Camillo,
Paulina, Lords, and Attendants.

Leon. O grave and good Paulina, the great comfort
That I have had of thee!
    Paul.   What, sovereign sir,
I did not well, I meant well. All my services
You have paid home: but that you have vouchsafed,   5
With your crowned brother and these your contracted
Heirs of your kingdoms, my poor house to visit,
It is a surplus of your grace, which never
My life may last to answer.
    Leon.   O Paulina,   10
We honor you with trouble: but we came
To see the statue of our queen. Your gallery
Have we passed through, not without much content
In many singularities; but we saw not
That which my daughter came to look upon,   15
The statue of her mother.
    Paul.   As she lived peerless,
So her dead likeness, I do well believe,

22. **mocked:** imitated.
26. **Comes it not something near:** does it not come close to her likeness.
27. **posture:** figure.

Excels whatever yet you looked upon
Or hand of man hath done; therefore I keep it   20
Lonely, apart. But here it is: prepare
To see the life as lively mocked as ever
Still sleep mocked death. Behold, and say 'tis well!
[*Paulina draws a curtain, and discovers Hermione
                              standing like a statue.*]
I like your silence, it the more shows off
Your wonder. But yet speak: first, you, my Liege.   25
Comes it not something near?
    Leon.   Her natural posture!
Chide me, dear stone, that I may say indeed
Thou art Hermione; or rather, thou art she
In thy not chiding, for she was as tender   30
As infancy and grace. But yet, Paulina,
Hermione was not so much wrinkled, nothing
So aged as this seems.
    Pol.   Oh, not by much.
    Paul. So much the more our carver's excellence;   35
Which lets go by some sixteen years and makes her
As she lived now.
    Leon.   As now she might have done,
So much to my good comfort, as it is
Now piercing to my soul. Oh, thus she stood,   40
Even with such life of majesty, warm life,
As now it coldly stands, when first I wooed her!
I am ashamed. Does not the stone rebuke me
For being more stone than it? O royal piece,
There's magic in thy majesty, which has   45
My evils conjured to remembrance, and

55. **fixed:** painted.

57-9. **your sorrow was too sore laid on,/ Which sixteen winters cannot blow away,/ So many summers dry:** your sorrow was felt so grievously that sixteen winters could not disperse it nor as many summers dry (exhaust) it.

65. **piece up:** make up for.

68. **wrought:** distressed.

From thy admiring daughter took the spirits,
Standing like stone with thee.
   Per.   And give me leave,
And do not say 'tis superstition that   50
I kneel and then implore her blessing. Lady,
Dear queen, that ended when I but began,
Give me that hand of yours to kiss.
   Paul.   Oh, patience!
The statue is but newly fixed, the color's   55
Not dry.
   Cam. My lord, your sorrow was too sore laid on,
Which sixteen winters cannot blow away,
So many summers dry. Scarce any joy
Did ever so long live; no sorrow   60
But killed itself much sooner.
   Pol.   Dear my brother,
Let him that was the cause of this have pow'r
To take off so much grief from you as he
Will piece up in himself.   65
   Paul.   Indeed, my lord,
If I had thought the sight of my poor image
Would thus have wrought you—for the stone is mine—
I'ld not have showed it.
   Leon.   Do not draw the curtain.   70
   Paul. No longer shall you gaze on't, lest your fancy
May think anon it moves.
   Leon.   Let be, let be.
Would I were dead, but that, methinks, already—
What was he that did make it? See, my lord,   75
Would you not deem it breathed? and that those veins
Did verily bear blood?

81. **As we are:** as though we were.
93. **cordial comfort:** comforting tonic.

Pol.   Masterly done:
The very life seems warm upon her lip.
 Leon. The fixture of her eye has motion in't,   80
As we are mocked with art.
 Paul.   I'll draw the curtain.
My lord's almost so far transported that
He'll think anon it lives.
 Leon.   O sweet Paulina,   85
Make me to think so twenty years together!
No settled senses of the world can match
The pleasure of that madness. Let't alone.
 Paul. I am sorry, sir, I have thus far stirred you: but
I could afflict you farther.   90
 Leon.   Do, Paulina;
For this affliction has a taste as sweet
As any cordial comfort. Still, methinks,
There is an air comes from her. What fine chisel
Could ever yet cut breath? Let no man mock me,   95
For I will kiss her.
 Paul.   Good my lord, forbear.
The ruddiness upon her lip is wet:
You'll mar it if you kiss it, stain your own
With oily painting. Shall I draw the curtain?   100
 Leon. No, not these twenty years.
 Per.   So long could I
Stand by, a looker-on.
 Paul.   Either forbear,
Quit presently the chapel, or resolve you   105
For more amazement. If you can behold it,
I'll make the statue move indeed, descend
And take you by the hand: but then you'll think,

Which I protest against, I am assisted
By wicked powers.   110
    Leon.   What you can make her do,
I am content to look on: what to speak,
I am content to hear; for 'tis as easy
To make her speak as move.
    Paul.   It is required   115
You do awake your faith. Then all stand still;
Or, those that think it is unlawful business
I am about, let them depart.
    Leon.   Proceed.
No foot shall stir.   120
    Paul.   Music, awake her; strike! [*Music.*]
'Tis time; descend; be stone no more; approach;
Strike all that look upon with marvel. Come,
I'll fill your grave up. Stir, nay, come away,
Bequeath to Death your numbness, for from him 125
Dear life redeems you. You perceive she stirs.
                   [*Hermione comes down.*]
Start not: her actions shall be holy as
You hear my spell is lawful. Do not shun her
Until you see her die again; for then
You kill her double. Nay, present your hand: 130
When she was young you wooed her; now in age
Is she become the suitor?
    Leon.   Oh, she's warm!
If this be magic, let it be an art
Lawful as eating.   135
    Pol.   She embraces him.
    Cam. She hangs about his neck.
If she pertain to life, let her speak too.

156. **issue:** outcome.
158. **upon this push:** at this point.
159. **like relation:** i.e., troublesome relation.
161. **Partake to:** share with.
164. **lost:** dead.

Pol. Ay, and make it manifest where she has lived,
Or how stol'n from the dead.   140
  Paul.   That she is living,
Were it but told you, should be hooted at
Like an old tale: but it appears she lives,
Though yet she speak not. Mark a little while.
Please you to interpose, fair madam: kneel   145
And pray your mother's blessing. Turn, good lady.
Our Perdita is found.
  Her.   You gods, look down,
And from your sacred vials pour your graces
Upon my daughter's head! Tell me, mine own,   150
Where hast thou been preserved? where lived? how
    found
Thy father's court? For thou shalt hear that I,
Knowing by Paulina that the oracle
Gave hope thou wast in being, have preserved   155
Myself to see the issue.
  Paul.   There's time enough for that,
Lest they desire upon this push to trouble
Your joys with like relation. Go together,
You precious winners all; your exultation   160
Partake to everyone. I, an old turtle,
Will wing me to some withered bough and there
My mate, that's never to be found again,
Lament till I am lost.
  Leon.   O, peace, Paulina!   165
Thou shouldst a husband take by my consent,
As I by thine a wife. This is a match,
And made between 's by vows. Thou hast found mine;
But how, is to be questioned; for I saw her,

175. richly noted: amply known; **justified:** confirmed.

As I thought, dead; and have in vain said many   170
A prayer upon her grave. I'll not seek far—
For him, I partly know his mind—to find thee
An honorable husband. Come, Camillo,
And take her by the hand, whose worth and honesty
Is richly noted and here justified   175
By us, a pair of kings. Let's from this place.
What! look upon my brother. Both your pardons,
That e'er I put between your holy looks
My ill suspicion. This your son-in-law
And son unto the King, whom, Heavens directing,   180
Is trothplight to your daughter. Good Paulina,
Lead us from hence, where we may leisurely
Each one demand and answer to his part
Performed in this wide gap of time since first
We were dissevered. Hastily lead away.   185

                                        Exeunt.

KEY TO

Famous Lines

A sad tale's best for winter.   [*Mamillius*—II. i. 34]

I am a feather for each wind that blows.
                         [*Leontes*—II. iii. 188]

When daffodils begin to peer,
With heigh! the doxy over the dale....   [*Song*—IV. iii. 1-14]

A snapper-up of unconsidered trifles.
                       [*Autolycus*—IV. iii. 27-8]

Jog on, jog on, the footpath way,
And merrily hent the stile-a....   [*Song*—IV. iii. 126-29]

Flora,/ Peering in April's front.   [*Florizel*—IV. iv. 2-3]

Nature is made better by no mean/ But nature
    makes that mean.   [*Polixenes*—IV. iv. 105-6]

    Daffodils,
That come before the swallow dares and take
The winds of March with beauty; violets, dim,
But sweeter than the lids of Juno's eyes. ...
                     [*Perdita*—IV. iv. 138-49]

When you do dance, I wish you/ A wave o' the sea,
    that you might ever do/ Nothing but that.
                  [*Florizel*—IV. iv. 162-63]

She is/ The queen of curds and cream.
                     [*Camillo*—IV. iv. 186-87]